MOONLIGHT IN MONTREAL

TRACY BROEMMER

Moonlight in Montreal

by

Tracy Broemmer

Contemporary Romance

Published by Tracy Broemmer

Edited by Lexie Broemmer

Cover Design by Amy Queau, Q Designs

Copyright © 2023

ISBN#: 978-1-95951637-62-0

Moonlight in Montreal deals with anxiety, depression, & how some people perceive the diagnoses as well as taking prescription medication for mental illnesses. I don't feel that the story is so harsh or emotional to demand trigger warnings. In fact, despite that heavy issue, I wanted to keep the story light and hopeful.

I know a lot of people right now dealing with anxiety, depression & other mental illnesses. And this story is my way of reminding all of us (myself included) that we're not alone and it's okay to do what it takes to heal.

This is for so many people. I won't list names, but if you're reading this, you know who you are.

CHAPTER 1

WELL, AT LEAST SHE DIDN'T GET UP AT THE CRACK OF dawn, shower, grab a taxi, and drag all her shit to the airport only to find out her flight was canceled. There was that anyway.

But there was also a massive weather event happening—blizzard-like conditions that had already dumped three feet of snow in the area with predictions for another twenty to thirty-five inches in the coming day or two.

Or hour, Tori Baker decided as she stared out the window of the coffeehouse.

"Damn damn damn," she muttered as she turned back to her laptop.

The worst part of it, though? It didn't matter.

There was nothing pressing at home—no boss tapping his foot wondering where the hell she was, no husband or kids to miss her, not even a damned dog at the kennel waiting for her to come and get him.

Interesting that it took a snowstorm in Montreal for Tori to see how meaningless her life had become. Well, no, not *meaningless*. But as of ten days ago, she was unemployed, and she was still feeling salty as hell over that.

Besides, she wanted to go home. She'd come here to visit her aunt, to lick her wounds after losing her job, and to regroup. She'd had a nice visit with Aunt Faith, and she had licked her wounds plenty—with salt and margaritas. Honestly, she wasn't sure what regrouping would entail. Seemed like more of a buzz word than a real concept. She hadn't found a way to get her old job back. Nor had she found a new job.

And now she was stuck in Montreal. If she wanted to freeze her ass off while being bummed out about losing her job, she was ready to do that in the comfort of her own home. She tapped a few keys on her laptop, irritated with herself when she automatically went to social media. Good grief, she was an adult. What the hell productive could come out of scrolling social media and reading stupid memes and bullshit news articles all morning? Again?

She could spend more time with her mother's younger sister, but Faith was a lot like her mom. Fun to hang out with. Maternal in *some* ways. But very busy with her own life and protective of her time and schedule.

"Excuse me."

Tori picked her mug up for a drink as she sat back in her chair.

"Ma'am?"

She had heard the guy the first time he spoke to her; she just wasn't in any hurry to see what he needed. With the heavy mug at her lips, Tori flicked her gaze over to the right of her table. A dude in joggers. She was not, never had been, a fan of joggers on guys. At least they weren't gray. Gray joggers or sweats on a guy weren't *bad,* but she'd rather not see that in public. Too much like a woman walking around in lingerie.

Slowly, Tori tipped her chin up and dragged her eyes over the guy's package—hard to miss it in the joggers, after all—his slim waist, wide shoulders, and finally his glowering face. What she could see of it, anyway, under his beard and thick, bushy eyebrows.

"What?" She arched an eyebrow at him and reached to close her laptop at the same time. Not that he was looking at her screen. Not that she cared if he saw that Ellen Magee posted more pictures of her cat. It was just habit, she supposed.

"Could I borrow your phone charger for a few minutes?"

Tori jerked her gaze from his and glanced at her phone next to the laptop on the table. And the cord plugged into it. The business end of the cord in the outlet to the left of her table. The guy had a regular cup in his hand; he wasn't planning to walk out with his coffee and her charger.

"Sure." She shrugged and leaned forward to tug the cord from the outlet. The guy heaved a dramatic sigh as he settled on a stool at the window bar. Tori eyed his backside and echoed his sigh. At least he didn't sit *directly* in front of her. Not that she had a great view anyway.

Snow. White stuff. A fuckton on the ground. More flakes of it falling. Not much traffic. Now and then a brave soul wandered by the window, bundled up against the bitterly cold wind. Kind of like a winter fashion show, maybe, since she was getting a good look at winter coats.

"Thank you," he mumbled as he took the charger from her and plugged the end into his phone.

She wasn't sure a few minutes of charging would do him much good, but he could knock himself out trying. Didn't matter to her a bit; she could sit here and stare at her laptop all day no matter whose phone her charger was plugged into.

Tori glanced at the guy again; he had put his phone face down on the bar. She could see his fingers wrapped around his cup; his fingernails were short, bitten to the quick. *Ouch*. She flinched and looked back at her computer. And naturally, eyed her own nails as she opened the laptop up again.

Her manicure was okay; she would be due for another one in a few more days. Then again, stuck in Montreal where she knew no one but her aunt, with no life on the home front, maybe she didn't need a manicure.

She tapped a few keys, exited out of her social media accounts, and typed in *reading literacy specialist*. Again. Disappointed, but not surprised that nothing new had popped up in the past ten minutes, she rested her elbows on the table and plopped her head in her hands.

"Tell me about it," the guy grumbled.

She looked his way, but before she could respond, his phone buzzed. And buzzed. When it appeared he had no intention of answering the call, she dropped her hands to her lap and leaned forward to see his face.

"Your phone's ringing," she told him. "You know? The one that you needed my charger for?"

The guy—she guessed him to be close to her age, give or take a year or two—clenched his teeth and nodded. Rolling his head on his neck, he picked the phone up, pulled the cord from it, and handed it back to her. Tori frowned, wondering if she had pissed him off.

He flipped the phone over, drilled his finger into the red hang up button, and then turned it off.

"Never mind." He peeked at her. "But thank you, anyway."

CHAPTER 2

Hudson

The dark roast coffee wasn't doing a damned thing to quell the jackhammer in his head. Should have just made it at home—strong enough to stand without a cup. Fuck that. Should have just stayed in bed. Again.

Hudson shoved his fingers into his eyes and rubbed hard. When he was a kid, he did this to see the kaleidoscope of colors. Now if he did it, it was a useless attempt at shoving his damned headaches away.

Wouldn't work. He knew it.

"Good God."

The softly spoken words sounded more like a curse than a prayer. Hudson let up on the pressure on his eyes and turned his head just a bit. The woman was still sitting there behind him. Her laptop was open again, but it looked like she was looking at him.

Of course she was going to be pissy about loaning him the damned charger and then watching him decline that call.

Decline. Hudson snorted softly. He'd throw the fucking thing in the Saint Lawrence River if his parents wouldn't unleash the dogs on him instantly. Being tied to them by phone was remotely better than house arrest.

"I didn't feel like talking to her," he muttered. Odds were the red head behind him wouldn't hear him, but he didn't care. He didn't have to explain himself to her. But maybe if he mumbled a bit, she would pack up and go. This window seat had been his for several months now. Who the hell was she to come in here and bat those blue eyes and act like she owned the damned place?

"I hate snow."

Not sure he heard her right, Hudson twisted a bit further to see her better. She wasn't looking at her laptop, but she wasn't looking at him, either. Instead, she was aiming a super pissed-off-looking frown at the window beside him and apparently cussing the snow.

"It's Montreal," he reminded her. "In the winter."

"No shit, genius," she grumbled. "It snows in other places, too. I hate it everywhere."

Hudson huffed a little laugh, amused by her observation. She didn't sound Canadian or French, and if she was grumbling about snow in other places, too, he assumed she was visiting.

"Be glad you don't live here." He turned back to the window and picked up his cup. The coffee was cold. He could leave it. Head back outside and walk back to his place. Sit around there and twiddle his thumbs while he waited for his fucking parental-parole check. He had some weed at home. They'd taken everything else—the coke, the hard liquor. Not even in a nice, just in case way. More of a control move so their youngest son couldn't embarrass them yet again.

Still, he did have the weed. And he had money. He could go buy whatever he needed.

He'd been clean, though, for a month. Not that he had a problem. His parents refused to listen to him about the weed —and he hadn't even touched that. Nope, for the past month, he had been trying his therapist's suggestions for coping with anxiety. Identifying triggers was easy—two major triggers being his parents and a third being his dumbass brother. But the meditation and journaling were bogus.

"If you hate it, why do you live here?"

Hudson cringed. He'd forgotten the woman was behind him. Rather than scare her away, his comments appeared to have the opposite effect. Just what he wanted to do and great for his anxiety—conversation with a stranger.

"If that's not the million-dollar question." He shook his head, refusing to look at her again.

"I live in Illinois." Oddly enough, the edge in her voice took the edge off his anxiety. Just slightly, but still.

"The great state of Illinois." He smirked, eyes still on the window. "Where how many former-governors are now enjoying prison digs?"

"Four went to jail," she answered simply. "Seven have been arrested or indicted."

"And why do you live in Illinois if you hate it?"

Her laugh was musical, loud in the coffee shop, and most definitely unexpected. He peeked at her over his shoulder, expecting to find her watching him. But her eyes were on her screen. The glare made it hard for him to make anything out on the screen, but he didn't care. He had no desire to read or look at anything over her shoulder. Not even if she was watching porn. He couldn't get it up right now if he wanted to.

Great problem to have in his early thirties.

"If that's not the million-dollar question," she repeated his words back to him. Hudson shot her a grin when she looked up at him and shrugged. She was cute. Too bad he'd lost his mojo. It happened from time to time with no warning. Hudson had no interest in love or marriage or families. But he liked sex, so the problem with his dick was a problem.

"If I gave you a plane ticket now, where would you go?"

"Nowhere, because all the damned flights are canceled because of the fuckton of snow out there. Are you blind?"

Hudson spun around on his stool, chuckling as he did. He liked her. She had spunk. He'd heard that about red heads, but he tended to disregard anything his brother told him.

"I'm not blind." He tipped his head at her and raised his eyebrows. "It was more of a...hypothetical...question. Because not only are there no flights taking off right now, I'm not gonna hand you a plane ticket, either."

"Oh, so we're playing a game." She turned sideways and rested her elbow on the table.

Hudson considered and finally nodded. "Yeah. You got something better to do?"

The woman took a deep breath, puffed up like she was going to say something self-important, and then laughed and shook her head.

"No. I don't."

"I'm Hudson."

"Tori."

CHAPTER 3

TORI

"Tori," the guy said with a nod. "Where would you go?"

"Kamari Beach in Santorini," she answered immediately.

"Specific."

If he would trim the rangy bush growing on his face, he might be cute. She wasn't sure. Still, though, the joggers were unforgivable.

"The sand's black. From volcanic activity—"

He cut her off with a nod. "I know."

"Been there?"

"Not to Kamari Beach, but yeah. I've been to Santorini." He reached for his cup, plucked it up with an awkward grab, and took a drink. Tori laughed softly at the face he made. "It's cold."

"Want a warm-up?"

"I can get it."

"I wasn't offering."

He tipped his head back for a full throttle laugh and finally looked back at her with a nod.

"Why there?"

"The beach or Santorini?" She scooted her chair back just enough to turn fully sideways and look at him. The last thing she needed was a backache from sitting weird in the chair.

He shrugged. "Both?"

"Well, I doubt they're having a blizzard right now."

His grin was so big, so real, Tori thought his eyes twinkled.

"Yeah, but Mexico probably isn't, either."

She chuckled and shook her head. "Where would you go?"

"You didn't answer my question."

"I did." She nodded. "Maybe you were hoping for some fun, drunken story or even a sexy getaway story, but my main reason is that the likelihood of them getting this same snowstorm is pretty nonexistent."

"And would you stay there? If you were there? Or fly home?"

"You're perceptive," she said with a slow smile. Tucking her chin to her chest, she turned and picked up her cup for a drink.

"Why would you want to be in Santorini only so you could fly home?" He scooted off the stool and reached for her cup. "Want a warm-up?"

"Thank you." She handed him her cup and told herself she would not turn, she would not look at his ass, as he walked away. She would simply sit and count slowly until he returned. She hit two before she turned to watch him.

Still not a fan of joggers, but he did have a nice ass. It would look much better in denim or khakis. He poured refills in both cups and then sauntered back to the table.

"Thanks." She took her cup and blew on it. Hudson nodded to the chair across from her.

"Mind if I sit there?"

"Nope."

He sighed as he pulled the chair out to sit down. Under what didn't appear to be a heavy coat, he wore a hoodie. Leather high-top tennis shoes. Odds were, he was a diamond in the rough and might cleanup to be a good-looking guy.

Not that it mattered.

"I would go south."

"Belize?"

"Nashville," he answered deadpan.

"Why Nashville? Are you a star waiting to be born?"

That grin again. A little bit devilish, little bit charming. Tori cleared her throat and took a sip of her coffee.

"No, I'm not. But I lived there for a bit before coming here. I'd like to go back."

"I want to go home because I'm a control freak. I have nothing pressing that I need to get home to, but it makes me nuts that I was supposed to fly home today and can't."

"You can't just relax and enjoy another day or two here?"

"No." She shrugged. "I can't. It's snowing, Hudson. What's to enjoy about that?"

"You could go to the top of Mount Royal," he offered. "Great view from there."

Tori caved an inch and nodded. "I'm sure it's beautiful."

"Do you ski? Ice skate?"

"Do you?"

Hudson laughed and turned to look out the window. "I can. But I don't."

"I can ski. Not great on ice skates," she told him.

"Nothing to go home to?"

She quirked an eyebrow at him at the more personal question.

"No." She pressed her lips together and then dipped her chin and rubbed the bridge of her nose with her fingers. "I'm a reading literacy specialist, and I lost my job right before this trip. Budget cuts. I mean, I get that money's tight everywhere, but literacy's pretty important."

"Mm." He nodded. "Agreed. Interesting how music departments and humanities take the brunt of the budget cuts, isn't it? You never see funding pulled from STEM or sports programs."

"That's un-American." She laughed softly. "Watch yourself, Hudson. You might get arrested for treason."

"We're in Canada," he reminded her dryly.

"What do you do?" she asked him, sincerely interested.

He flinched and looked away, leaning over to rest his elbows on his knees. "Nothing. Right now, I am doing nothing. I am the family fuckup, and even if I were a neurosurgeon, I would be the family fuckup, because I'm not my brother."

With a frown, Tori raked her gaze over his face, noting the dull look in his eyes and the downturn of his lips. He looked tense now, when moments before he was splayed out in the chair, laughing with her.

"Well, now," she said quietly. "That's a lot to unpack."

"Nah, I never pack my shit up. It's just out there."

She stared at him boldly for a moment, relieved when his face finally broke into a grin.

"I feel like we need something stronger than coffee," she mumbled.

"Funny." He shook his head. "Someone would blow the whistle on me, and even though I am thirty-two years old, my parents would send their people for me and throw me into rehab."

"You're an alcoholic?"

"I'm not. But it's easier for my parents to believe that than the truth."

"And what's the truth?"

"I do drink a lot," he said with a shrug. "Sometimes. I self-medicate because I'm fucked up. They raised me. They don't like the implications."

Tori nodded, but she was quiet, thinking about what he had said.

"And you have just the one brother?"

"I do."

"What's he do? Is he a doctor? An astronaut?"

Hudson's harsh, sarcastic laugh made her shiver.

"St. Liam is a professional athlete."

She flinched at the sarcasm this time.

"Hockey?"

"Good guess, but no," he answered with a sardonic grin. "Soccer."

"Interesting," she said softly. "And are you a musician?"

Maybe that would explain his beef with funding always going to sports programs instead of music.

"No. Learned to play the recorder in sixth grade." He shifted in the chair again and avoided her eyes. "So did St. Liam, by the way. I played soccer, too. And I played basketball as a kid. I was good. But not as good as Liam."

"Got it." She nodded.

Hudson took a drink, eyes still on the window, on the snow outside.

"You?"

"I do not play soccer," she answered. "Or basketball. I played volleyball in high school. I'm not a musician, but yes, I did learn to play *Three Blind Mice* on the recorder. It's such a well-rounded skill."

He flicked his eyes to her and grinned at her over his cup.

"Brothers or sisters?"

"No, though at times, my dad seems to think we're sisters and not father and daughter."

Hudson cocked an eyebrow at her.

"What's that look like?"

CHAPTER 4

HUDSON

Across the table, Tori heaved a big sigh, leaned back, and dropped her arms to let her hands hang down beside her chair.

"Oh God. Sometimes, it's ugly." She closed her eyes for a second, opened them, and then shook her head as if to scatter her thoughts. "I don't know how or why my parents ever married."

"So, they're divorced?"

"Yes." She nodded. "They divorced when I was fourteen. They're nothing alike. I don't think they have *anything* in common. My mom runs her own business. She has for years. She's great, but she's not always real touchy feely maternal-like. My dad is a playboy. I mean, if he weren't my dad, I'd say he a was a tool."

"So, they must have had great sex." Hudson shrugged.

"Oh God." She squeezed her eyes closed and bit her lip. "Thanks for that, Hudson."

"How does your dad think he's your sister?"

"He's like a best girlfriend. He's like what my *mom* should be. Calls me almost every day. Tells me about a sale he hit. New shoes he found. New car. New girlfriend. Shares stuff they did on their date. Asks me questions like that." She shivered. "I mean...it's weird, but it's...Dad. And Mom's Mom."

"Weird family dynamic," Hudson offered.

"That's exactly it," she agreed.

"That works for you."

"It does work for us." She nodded and drummed her fingers on the table. "But when I think about it, I just wonder *how* it works."

"Do they speak to each other?"

"Yeah. They're good friends, I guess. It's hard to be close to Mom, but she's got a soft spot for him. Her sister seems to think he's the devil in disguise."

"Wanna go for a walk?"

"What?"

"A walk."

"It's snowing."

"Mmm." He nodded and looked toward the windows. "Where I come from—"

"Which is where?"

"Michigan. We actually did things outside when it snowed. I thought people from Illinois did, too."

"You," she leaned around the table to give him a once over and then hit him square in the face with a bold look, "want to go for a walk. In the snow. In those shoes."

"I can grab boots at my apartment."

"Grab boots at your apartment," she repeated quietly.

"And you could leave your stuff there." He aimed his gaze at her laptop now.

"Where in particular do you want to walk?"

"No destination in mind." He pulled in a deep breath and let it out slowly. "I need to move."

Tori studied him curiously for a moment and finally nodded. "Sure, I'll go for a walk in a blizzard with you."

"That's the spirit," he said with a grin. Tori slapped her laptop closed, tucked it in a messenger bag, and then slipped her phone in the bag, too. "Don't forget this."

She smiled when he handed her the charger. He wouldn't have asked her to go for a walk, but he was feeling antsy, fidgety, and moving would help. But, on the other hand, he wasn't in a hurry to run her off anymore. She was funny; this was the most interesting conversation he'd had with anyone in ages. The invitation to walk would prolong it. And he had noticed she did have boots on.

They stood at the same time. Hudson watched her pull her long wool coat on and button it up. She eyed the open zipper of his coat pointedly. He ignored her just as pointedly. Finally, Tori slung the strap of her bag over her shoulder and nodded for him to lead on.

"See ya, Jones!"

Hudson bristled when the barista called after him at the door. He threw a hand in the air and waved, but he didn't look back. Outside, a knife of cold wind sliced his throat and ruffled his hair. He had a stocking cap, but he'd left it at home. Gloves, too. Also at home. Beside him, Tori tugged on her own beanie; damned if it didn't frame her face just right. A few red curls peeked out from under it. Her cheekbones were high, well-defined, and something about the beanie made her eyes pop.

Hudson looked away as she pulled gloves from her pockets and yanked them over her hands.

"Do you not know how to dress for winter?" she asked him after a few moments. "How long have you lived in Montreal?"

"About seventeen months," he answered. He didn't add that he hated it here, and therefore, he childishly refused to embrace anything about it, including the weather.

"So. You're from Michigan."

He nodded when he saw her peek up at him for confirmation.

"Born there?"

"Yep."

"And then you lived in Nashville. And now you live in Montreal."

"Lived in Chicago. Columbus, Ohio. Philly. I went to college at a small private school in Tennessee. Moved back to Philly for a bit after I graduated. Remembered why I hated living near my family so much and moved to Nashville."

"And now Montreal."

"And now Montreal."

The puzzled frown on her face amused him. Hudson watched her as they walked, picturing the wheels spinning in her head.

"What're you trying to figure out?"

She laughed softly. "The common thread. Like...military?"

"Soccer."

"Oh." She nodded.

"I messed up in Nashville. I did tell you I was the family fuckup," he reminded her. "Things were kind of ugly. My parents demanded my presence here."

"Even though you're an adult."

"Even though." He nodded dismissively. Not ready to dump all his fuckups and his parents' reprimands and ultimatums on her, he changed the subject. "Do you like museums?"

"You're giving me whiplash." She elbowed him in the side and laughed when he responded with an overly dramatic frown. "I do. Like museums."

"Art?"

"Art museums?"

"Mm-hmm."

"Oh no! Wait!" Excited by the new idea he'd just thought of, Hudson grabbed her by the elbow and slowed her down.

"Whiplash." Her whisper made him laugh.

"C'mon. This is great." He tugged at her, and she started walking again.

"What about your apartment? Your boots?"

"Eh. My feet will get wet." He shrugged. "I'll live."

Tori looked up at him as they walked. Hudson laughed when she rolled her eyes and shook her head.

"What?"

"You are like a puppy." She eyed him again and looked away.

"Is that a nice way of saying I'm obnoxious?"

"I wouldn't say you're obnoxious," she hedged. "You just have a lot of energy."

"It's okay. My parents tell me daily how obnoxious I am."

"I don't think I like your parents much."

"I don't. Like them." He shrugged.

"So. Where are we going?"

"Museum of Illusions."

"Mm. Okay." She nodded. "Sounds interesting."

"And we could do the Museum of Fine Art."

"Sure."

"And then maybe ice-fishing."

"Yeah, no. I don't go fishing when it's *not* cold."

"Just making sure you're listening."

The look she gave him—a little bit coy and sort of sweet— made his ribs get two times smaller. Hudson coughed to catch his breath.

"I always listen."

"Most people don't want to listen to me too long." He remembered suddenly that she was carrying her laptop, and he had told her she could stash it as his apartment. "Here. Let me carry that for you."

"How do I know you're not gonna take off at a dead run and steal it?"

Hudson chuckled. "Well, for one thing, it looks ancient, so it might end up costing me more than just buying a new one. And second, I have a new laptop at home. And third, I don't want your laptop. I just think you're fun."

The frown on her face almost made him panic. Had he said too much? Too sarcastic? Or too serious? But when she glanced at him this time, she wore a small smile. And damned if her eyes weren't twinkling.

"Thank you," she said softly. "You don't have to carry my bag."

"I don't mind."

CHAPTER 5

TORI

"So, what were you doing in Montreal? Before you got snowed in and your flight was canceled?"

"Visiting my aunt." She ducked her head against the wind as they turned a corner.

"For the holidays?"

"Did the holidays happen?" she asked with a laugh.

"You don't do Christmas?"

"Most of the time." Hunching her shoulders against the cold, Tori thought about her recent Christmases. All of them, really, had been good. Even with the weird family dynamic. None of them had been traditional, not even before her parents divorced. But she couldn't complain. "But this year was just different."

"Recent breakup?"

"Hmm?" She looked up at him quickly and shook her head. "No. It's the job. I've been stewing over it."

"Got it."

"I'm not destitute, and I'll take a job before it would ever come to that."

"But?"

"I was comfortable there. I liked my coworkers. I loved the kids I worked with. I was seeing improvements with most of them, and it just makes me angry that someone in a high-up office can eyeball a ledger or a computer screen and start making budget cuts. No, maybe those cuts don't affect them, but those poor kids need that extra help."

"It does affect the people in the high-up offices, though, doesn't it? Today's kids will run tomorrow's world."

Surprised by Hudson's insight, Tori scanned the block ahead and nodded.

"True."

"Where does your aunt live?"

"She actually lives in Quebec City. I took the train and stayed with her for a couple of days."

Hudson quirked an eyebrow. She laughed; he was dying to ask questions but apparently, he didn't want to be nosy.

"She's my mom's sister," she explained, still wearing a big grin. What was she smiling about? She had lost her job. She missed her friends, the students she worked with. She didn't have any hope of finding a job in her field in Illinois. It was snowing cats and dogs, and she was stuck in a hotel in Montreal for who knew how long?

She was smiling because of Hudson. He was fun.

"And being your mom's sister..." He tipped his head, eyes on her face, waiting for a clue.

"She's great. But she's—she's busy. She has her life, and she'll spend time with you if she can pencil it in. Neither Mom nor Aunt Faith is spontaneous."

"So, staying at her place until you can fly back is out of the question."

"I suppose I could contact her and ask if I could come stay. She would say yes, but I would feel like I was in her way."

"Hmm." Hudson mulled that over. "Well, if you were planning to stay with her, you couldn't hang out with me."

"Good point."

"You're gonna love this museum."

Their eyes met. She was freezing. Her bones ached; she was so damned cold. And yes, she was still frustrated to be here instead of at home, but she had a feeling she was going to love the museum. Not because of anything she might see there, but because she was hanging out with Hudson.

"This it?" She nodded ahead at the building in front of them.

"Yep." He pulled a wallet from his coat pocket and fished a bill from it.

"You don't have to pay my way."

"I know." He shrugged. "But I will. I asked you to come here."

* * *

THE MUSEUM OF ILLUSIONS was a fun way to kill some time on a blustery, snowy winter day. Tori wasn't sure she would have enjoyed it half as much if she weren't with Hudson. They laughed together as they made their way through the chambers of illusions. But the Clone table, the Beuchet chair, and the Head on a platter experiences were their favorites. Hudson was like a little kid, shifting around on his feet and sighing dramatically as Tori read everything there was to read about each illusion and experience.

It took them a little over an hour to go through the place. Tori loved seeing the families here, watching the kids and parents alike have their minds blown. She wasn't in any big hurry to leave the place, considering it was warm inside and still snowing outside. But she didn't particularly want to go straight to the Museum of Fine Arts, either. She knew it would also be an expensive ticket to buy, and she suspected Hudson would insist on buying hers again.

"I know how you can pay me back," he said as they left the building.

Tori shot him a look of warning, thrilled when he laughed at her.

"Get your mind out of the gutter." He shook his head. "Buy me lunch."

"So, that's it."

"What?" He stayed behind for a second to hold the door open for a young couple.

"Your angle."

"What's my angle?" He shook his head as he hurried out after her.

"Hittin' me up for my charger. Only to not answer the *one* phone call you got. Askin' me to come here. Charming me by carrying my bag. Just so I would buy you lunch."

He shrugged and arched his eyebrows. "You figured me out. It's been too long since I've had lunch with a pretty girl."

She laughed and rolled her eyes.

"I didn't want your charger because I was expecting a phone call."

"No?" She looked up at him as they walked. "Oh. I know! You were reading a good book on Kindle, and you didn't want your phone to die and leave you hanging."

"No." He shook his head. "Guess again."

"Expecting a text from your girlfriend."

"Fishing," he pointed at her with a look of suspicion, "but, no."

"I give."

"Playing Crazy Kitchen Cookin'."

Tori stopped walking and stared at him with a frown. "What?"

Hudson looked back at her for a moment and finally shook his head.

"You heard me." He took off walking again, and she scrambled to catch up with him.

"A game. You were playing a game on your phone, and you needed my charger," she said with a nod, as if she understood his need.

"Yep."

"A cooking game." She giggled.

"Stop it." He swung his hip into her gently as they continued walking.

"So, was the phone call some rando doing political polls or someone trying to sell you credit card protection?"

"How would I know? I didn't answer it."

"Yeah, but you know how it is. Those calls come from the same damned numbers day after day after day."

He nodded his head back and forth and stared straight ahead.

"It was my mom."

CHAPTER 6

HUDSON

They ducked into a pub halfway down the block. Hudson had never been inside, but he knew without a doubt it would be warmer than walking, and Tori was shivering. She hadn't complained, nothing other than the grumbling about the snow before they started out on their walk. But he could tell she was cold, and he was ready to sit down somewhere warm, too.

And talk to her.

He didn't care where they were. As long as their rambling conversation continued, he was good with it.

Tori stood frozen just inside the door. Hudson nearly plowed her over when he stepped inside. Hovering over her shoulder, he looked around the shadowy interior, wondering if something was wrong.

"What?" he finally asked when he saw nothing out of the ordinary.

"Hmm?"

"What're you doing? Is something wrong?"

"No." She shivered again. Hudson, standing so close to her, breathed in her sweet, rich scent. He eyed the back of her head; she still wore the beanie. Her neck was hidden by the collar of her coat, but the scent of what he assumed was her perfume, made him want to touch her skin. Maybe just press his fingertips to the pulse point under her ear. Nuzzle his nose over the back of her neck.

His dick stirred. Hudson caught himself before he tipped his head down to gape at his groin in surprise. He wasn't sure when that last happened—getting a hard-on just standing close to a woman and thinking about her skin.

"I'm just reveling in the heat." She looked at him over her shoulder. Her blue eyes had that twinkle again, her smile lit up the dark pub.

"Me, too." He nodded, wishing now that he could adjust himself. Why had he worn the joggers today? On the other hand, he hadn't been turned on by much of anything in so long, it never crossed his mind it could be a problem.

"Seat yourself!" A bald man behind the big wooden bar in the center of the pub called. He waved his hand around the place to indicate a number of open tables. Hudson nodded and waved back in appreciation.

"Are you done reveling?" he asked.

Her sweet, musical laughter trailed after her as she led the way to a booth midway into the room.

"This okay?" She looked at him when she stopped. "Away from the door but not by the restrooms."

Hudson laughed and nodded. "This is good."

He set her bag on the table, shrugged out of his coat, and tossed it on the seat. He waited while she unbuttoned her coat and then stepped behind her to help her shrug it off. He was not a fan of his parents, but at the moment, he was glad they had instilled manners and chivalry in him. Even if some women wanted chivalry to be dead, Hudson didn't see the harm in offering a woman a hand with simple things.

"Thank you," she murmured as she took the coat back from him and put it on her seat. She grabbed her bag as she sat down and put it on her coat and then reached up to pull the beanie off. Hudson sat down across the table, unable to take his eyes from her. She fluffed up her curls, dropped the beanie on her bag, and reached for a menu. "What's good here?"

"No idea."

"You live here."

"Have you been to every bar in Illinois?"

Eyes still on the menu, she snorted softly and shook her head. "Not for lack of trying."

"Tori's a party girl." He sat back and tipped his head to study her. Her cheeks were still pink with the cold, her eyes bright and happy. Compared to the girls he had dated recently—well, okay, not recently, because he hadn't gone out for a while— Tori was a breath of fresh air.

"Ha." She rolled her eyes. "If by party, you mean curl up in bed with a good book by nine most nights, then yes, I am a party girl."

"What about the bars? The trying thing?"

She pursed her lips and nodded her head from side to side. "Eh. Well. I go out with the girls sometimes, but I like my time at home."

"No boyfriend?"

"Fishing." She pointed at him over the menu.

"You can't call fishing, when I obviously just asked you if you have a boyfriend."

"True." She nodded and frowned down at her menu.

"That's not an answer, by the way."

"No boyfriend." She shook her head. "The last guy I went out with was into coin collecting."

"And you're not?"

"Well, I mean, if I'm dating someone who has a hobby, sure I wanna know about it. Ya know? But no, it's not something I want to spend all my time talking about."

"Noted."

"Lemme guess." She tipped the menu her way and grinned at him. "You were about to start rattling to me about your rare stamp collection."

"Is this a date?" He threw the words out as a challenge, happy when she laughed again.

"A day date in Montreal."

Hudson quirked an eyebrow at her.

"There are worse things," she decided.

"Than going out with me?"

"Than a day date in snowy Montreal with you."

"Tell me one."

"What?" She closed her menu with a giggle.

"Tell me one thing worse than a day date in snowy Montreal with me."

"Sitting in that coffee shop alone today, staring out the window, and watching the snow fall."

Hudson pursed his lips and shook his head.

"What?"

"You hate snow. We've established that. I would hope that would be worse than spending the day with me."

"Hmm. Okay. You're right." She nodded. Menu forgotten now, Hudson watched her drum her fingers on the table. "Being on any sort of date with any of the guys I've been out with. Recently."

"Recently? You had to add that caveat?"

"Well, I mean, I have had some pretty great dates. I'm not a spring chicken, Hudson."

"Right. You must be all of twenty-five."

"Ha." She laughed and pointed at him again. "You're not gettin' brownie points to make me remove the caveat."

Hudson shrugged.

"Thirty-two," she corrected him. "And I..." She shrugged and cocked her head with a smile. "I've had some good dates."

"Okay." He nodded. "I'll be happy with this being better than any of your *recent* dates."

CHAPTER 7

TORI

"So." Tori sighed as she watched the waiter walk away from the table. They'd both ordered burgers, fries, and colas. She wouldn't have minded a beer with her burger, but if Hudson was seriously having a problem with his drinking, she didn't want to make it worse. Across the table, Hudson was reading a sign on the wall over their table.

"Did you like the museum?"

"I did." She nodded. "Pretty cool."

"Good. We can do the art museum, but I thought that would be fun. I don't think it's been open very long."

"What do you do?" she asked him.

"I fuck up." He fiddled with the salt and pepper shaker. "Told you that."

"Yes, but did you study fucking up in college?"

Hudson laughed. "I fucked up and down and sideways in college."

"Not touching that," she said quietly. Hiding her amused smile behind her hand, Tori shook her head.

"I studied accounting," he told her. With a huff, as if to signify how bored he was by the turn in conversation, he flopped back in the booth and stared at her.

"Well, there's your problem."

"Hey, I didn't judge your literacy career," he reminded her.

"True. Sorry." She winced, chagrined by his comment. "I just don't love math. Of any sort."

"I don't know if I love it, but I'm good at it."

"But you're not working?" she asked.

"What gives you that idea?"

"That you were bumming my charger in a coffee shop this morning—correct me if I'm wrong, but it is Monday, isn't it? So you needed my charger to play a cooking game on your phone. And now you're playing handsome tour guide for me in this lovely Montreal snowstorm, instead of being at an office."

"You think I'm handsome?" Still relaxed in the booth, he quirked an eyebrow at her, his lips curving in a slight smile.

"Hudson, you think you're handsome." She rolled her eyes. "Don't think I can't read your vibe."

"Are you saying I'm cocky?"

She narrowed her eyes in thought for a moment and finally lifted a shoulder in a lazy shrug. "Charming? Maybe?"

"Well, it means a lot when a pretty woman says you're handsome. That's all."

Eyes locked, they sat quietly for a moment, only to look away when the waiter returned with their sodas.

"So, I was in an accounting position."

"In Nashville?"

"Yes. And I lost that job. Things got ugly. And so here I am."

"Fill in the blanks."

"If I fill in the blanks, you may decide you don't want to spend the rest of the day with me."

"Are you a serial killer?"

"No."

"Do you like animals?"

"I do."

"Pretty sure you're safe," she announced. Hudson watched her unwrap her straw and stick it in her glass before taking a drink. "But I get it if you don't want to share."

"Liam Jones."

Tori scanned her brain, her memory, but the name meant nothing to her.

"Don't know him."

"My brother."

"Oh." She flinched and wondered if she should feel guilty. At this point, she would align her allegiance with Hudson, but then again, what were they teaming up for? This was a one day hangout. "I don't follow professional soccer."

"I get it." Hudson nodded. "He's good."

"Okay."

"He's also an arrogant prick."

Hudson's words, his tone, were deadly sharp, but the look in his eyes was more disappointment than hatred.

"But," he held up a hand and offered her a sarcastic smile, "anything he does, it's okay. Most of the time, it's better than okay. He's an incredible human being. I'm a lot like Liam, but I'm a fuckup."

The obvious thing for her to say, what Tori wanted to say now, was what things had Liam done that were incredible, but were counted as fuckups for Hudson. But she didn't want to pressure him.

"Were you ever close to him?"

"When we were little kids," Hudson said with a quick nod. "He's two years older than me. I think we were eight and six, maybe, give or take, when it became clear that he was gifted."

"In school?"

"Soccer."

"Okay." She nodded, eyes on the door over Hudson's shoulder, so she didn't seem too eager for him to spill his guts.

"If I scored two goals in a game, Liam would score three. If I had a save as a goalie, Liam would play goalie and have an incredible, game-winning save."

"And was he an arrogant prick at that time?"

"Nah." Hudson shook his head. "That didn't start until we were in junior high."

"I have a cousin who was a country fair queen," she announced out of the blue. The silence had built between them again. Tension had crept into Hudson's neck and shoulders again, and he looked like he could snap his fork in two.

Maybe with his teeth.

She wanted to soothe him, but it didn't seem appropriate to climb over the table to his side of the booth to kiss his cheek. Or even to reach out and touch his hand. So she decided to share information. Her situation with her family was nothing like his, but they were talking. Conversing. Meaning, she couldn't expect Hudson to sit here and tell her his life story. She didn't want that. She wasn't a priest to hear confessions or a therapist to guide someone out of personal problems. Some of her exes had apparently mistaken her for both at times.

"Yeah? And was she pretty?"

"Very." Tori nodded. "I was eight. She was seventeen. On my dad's side of the family."

"Cool."

"It was," she agreed. "But then I went through a faze when I wanted to be a beauty queen."

"Like the pageants and stuff?"

"Yep. My mom had a fit. My dad thought it was the greatest thing ever."

"Did you compete?"

"Once. When I was ten. I'm not delicate. Or ladylike. At that time, especially, I was a bit more of a bull in a China shop. I had an awkward haircut. Bangs—it was terrible. And my mom got mascara in my eye. It watered so badly, I walked on stage with what looked like a black eye."

Hudson stared at her for a long moment, like he wasn't sure he believed her.

"And if I were to call your mother right now and ask her about this, would she say yes, that it happened?"

"She would, after she gave me a piece of her mind for giving you her phone number, because she's busy."

"I'm still not convinced."

"How can you not be convinced?" She lifted her arms from her sides and looked down at herself. "This is the same body I was working with."

"Well, no not if you were ten." He raked his gaze over her face and her shoulders and then jerked his eyes back up to hers again. "And yet, still, I would totally vote for you in any beauty pageant now."

She snorted and ducked her face to cover it with her hands. "No."

"No, it didn't happen?"

"Oh, it happened." She nodded as she dropped her hands to her lap. "And that's when I turned into a book nerd."

CHAPTER 8

HUDSON

Something about the way she damned near crushed the whole burger did something to him. Sure, she had cut it in half, and she was cute, girly, when she ate it. She would take a bite, set it down, and wipe her hands and mouth with a napkin. Hudson was too hungry to take that long. Still, though, Tori ate every last bite of her burger, and when he reached for her last fry, she laughed and pushed his hand away.

So many girls didn't eat when they were with guys. Hudson had seen it over and over. Girls wanting to be thin. Or girls not eating meat. Or whatever. He understood body dysmorphia. He understood the hateful things one person said to another could leave deep scars. It made him sad. And it made him happy to see people, women, like Tori, enjoy something.

"That was really good." She giggled as she wiped her mouth a final time. "I was hungry."

His mom would frown on the way Tori had eaten the whole thing. His dad would probably make some comment about wondering where she put it. Hudson wouldn't say a word, because he knew even a comment like that could be taken the wrong way and used as a weapon to inflict harm.

His meds made him such a wreck. Sometimes he couldn't eat anything without feeling sick immediately and dashing for the bathroom. And at other times, he wasn't remotely hungry. His parents ripped at him about both situations, making family dinners unbearable.

"It was good," he agreed. "The only possible thing to make it better would have been having a cold beer with it."

"Definitely."

"Why didn't you order one?"

Tori opened and closed her mouth without saying a word. Was she worried about triggering him? Angered by her assumption, and yet aware that he hadn't given her enough information, Hudson clenched his jaw and waited for her to answer.

"I just...I didn't need one." She shrugged.

"I'm not an alcoholic," he promised her. "And I'm also very aware now that you're probably thinking I must be an alcoholic because I've protested too much."

She shot him a grin. "You've read *MacBeth*."

"Hasn't everyone read *MacBeth* in high school?"

"Do you like Shakespeare?"

"Not particularly, no."

"Do you like to read?"

"Stats. Biographies."

"Okay." She nodded. "That's cool."

"Anyway, I just want you to know that. I have had occasions when I've had too much to drink, but I don't drink all the time."

"Did you lose your license?"

"No." He snorted softly. "Surprisingly, no. And if you want to have a beer now, I don't care."

"We just ate."

"Right, but people often sit in pubs and talk over beers."

"Are you saying you want to have a beer now?" She tipped her head quizzically.

"Not necessarily."

"But we need to order something else to stay here." She looked around. The pub was not remotely busy, so they could probably get away with not ordering anything and sticking around for a bit. But that felt sneaky to Hudson.

"Or we could go find a park and build a snowman."

"My favorite thing in the world to do," she mumbled with a groan.

"My favorite thing in the world to do is hiking."

"In the snow?"

"No. Just hiking. Biking. I love to be outside."

"Are your feet soaked?"

"A bit, yes."

"I'm sorry. That's miserable."

"I'll live."

"You could get frostbite."

He laughed, surprised when Tori waved their waiter down and ordered a draft beer. Hudson nodded when the waiter looked at him in askance.

"What was your talent?"

"What?"

"When you did the beauty pageant. Don't you have to do a talent?"

"Oh." She smiled and nodded. "Played 'Love Me Tender' on my dad's guitar."

"Elvis?"

"I wasn't incredibly talented on the guitar, and I think it was pretty butchered and unrecognizable. But yes, Elvis."

"I prefer Elvis Costello."

"Name one Elvis Costello song."

"What? You think I'm just being difficult?"

She laughed and nodded. "Kind of, yes."

"I have two vinyls at my apartment. *Spike* and *King of America*."

"But you didn't take me there, so I think you are lying."

Hudson held his hands up in defense, laughing heartily now. "No, I'm not. At some point today, I will take you there and show you."

"Mm-hmm."

"How about this? At some point, we can go to my apartment. I'll fix you dinner. And you can listen to Elvis Costello."

"Dinner? You cook?"

"I play a cooking game." He rolled his eyes.

"Uh yeah. Well, I played *Angry Birds* for a while. It didn't make me...an...angry bird."

"I dare you to come over and let me cook for you." He narrowed his eyes at her.

"Okay, fine."

Hudson knocked his fist on the table as he climbed to his feet.

"I gotta hit the little boys' room."

He slipped away from the table as the waiter carried their pint glasses over and set them down. The men's room was empty. Hudson took his time. While he did need the restroom after two cups of coffee earlier and the soda and burger now, he also needed a minute to himself.

Who was this woman? Tori. Tori, the blue-eyed redhead that made his heart beat a little faster. She made him laugh. She made him want a lot of things that he hadn't thought about for a long time.

He zipped up and washed his hands with barely a glance at himself in the mirror. Stopping to look into his own eyes would be dangerous. He didn't want to be reminded of who he was, that a slacker like him had no chance with a woman like Tori. For just one day, he would let himself pretend anything was possible.

CHAPTER 9

TORI

She nodded a thank you to the waiter as she dug her phone from her purse. A missed call from her dad. That could be interesting. She considered waiting to call him back. Sipped the draft beer while she thought about it, finger hovering over the screen. Finally, she tapped the redial button and put the phone to her ear.

Music played in the pub, but the words were all in French, so she had no idea what they were saying. Even if she did recognize the tune. Her dad answered on the second ring, and she instantly pushed the song from her mind.

"Hey Dad."

"Tori." He sounded excited to hear from her. She felt a smile cross her face as she wondered what he had to share with her today. "Are you home?"

"Nope. Snowed in."

"Where?"

"Montreal," she reminded him.

"That's right. You were visiting your mom's sister."

Her dad and Aunt Faith were not good friends, nor were they when her parents were married. Aunt Faith had no patience for his fashion and culture and girlfriends.

"I was. Supposed to fly home this morning. Looks like I'll be here for a few more days."

"Are you with Faith?" He sounded appropriately surprised, making Tori laugh a little.

"No. I came back to Montreal the day before yesterday. I've got a hotel room."

"Well, that sounds boring." He sighed as if he was frustrated for her. Before she could argue, tell him she'd met someone, he continued, "I hit the jackpot last night."

"Let me guess. Peter Millar sale? That doesn't seem likely."

"No, no." He laughed and mumbled something to someone else—probably his latest girlfriend. "I hit a jackpot."

"Oh. Vegas?"

"Yeah."

"Nice." She shook her head. "Did you blow it last night?"

"No. I did not. I bought Loni a necklace, but I actually saved most of it."

Loni.

Tori wracked her brain, but she didn't remember a Loni. The last one she had met was Lucy.

"That's cool."

"But yeah," he kept talking. "Heading to California tonight. We're going to wine country. Staying on her friend's estate."

Tori looked up as Hudson returned to the booth with a box in his hand. She smiled at him, frowned at the box until she realized it was a game, and then snapped her attention back to her dad.

"Have fun."

"Listen. Come out and join us."

"I can't."

"You can. I know you lost your job."

Tori flinched. She had talked to her mom, and though she would have told her dad, she was frustrated that her mom had already filled him in.

"Right. So I can't just traipse all over the world on a whim now," she reminded him. "I have pockets, but they're not that deep."

"Come out and stay for a week," he urged her. "My treat."

"Dad—"

She met Hudson's eyes as her dad cut her off.

"Seriously, Tori. It's cold at home. You're snowed in. I know you loved your job. Come out and warm up. Regroup."

Regroup. Well, she hadn't been successful at that yet. She was beginning to think in order to regroup, she would need to take a job in another field. Either that or leave home and relocate.

"Thanks, Dad."

"You'll think about it?"

"Sure."

She wouldn't. She was tired and ready to be home. And yes, she normally liked all her dad's girlfriends okay, but that didn't mean she wanted to spend a week with them anywhere.

"Okay. Hey, tell your mom Nordstrom had a denim blue platform sandal that would look incredible with her crème-colored pantsuit. Marked down."

"I will. Love you."

She might tell her mom, and she might not. But her mom wouldn't rush out buy them. Not like her dad would.

"Love you, too, baby girl."

Hudson was taking a drink when she ended the call and slipped her phone back in her bag.

"Did you call him?"

"Yeah."

She frowned, confused, when the slow grin crossed Hudson's face.

"What?"

"Lemme guess. Dad, I'm stuck in Montreal. I'm going to dinner tonight at some dude's apartment. Here's his name and DNA from a soda glass for you to run a background check."

Tori snorted. "Yes, I so cleverly took your DNA from your glass while you were sitting there, and you didn't see a thing."

"I wouldn't blame you," he said with a shrug. "If I had a sister, I would want to know if she were stuck somewhere and hanging out with a stranger." Before Tori could respond, Hudson harrumphed. "Well, maybe. If I had a sister, and she was anything like my parents or brother, I might feed her to the wolves."

"You wouldn't," she argued. "Any more than you would throw your brother or parents to wolves."

"And what makes you say that? Have I been unclear on how I feel about them?"

Tori stretched her fingers out and pulled the game Hudson had carried to the table closer. She eyed the box with interest, but she was thinking of how to phrase what she wanted to say.

"Mancala?"

"Do you play?"

"I can." She nodded.

"There's an Unsolved Case File game back there."

Tori laughed and shrugged. "Might be fun, but this is good." She kept her eyes on the box as she opened it and took the wooden board and mancala stones out. Hudson took another drink, as if he wasn't curious what she was thinking. But she could feel him watching her closely as she set the game up.

"So. I get that there's some major friction…issues…between you and your brother as well as you and your parents." She nodded, eyes still on the game. "And I understand that. And if you want to talk about it, I'm all ears. But also, we've been hanging out together for a few hours now. You've alluded to things, but you haven't said much. Which I take to mean that as much as you…dislike them?…as hard as things are for you right now, you don't hate them. Maybe you even wish things were different."

She met his eyes and stared at him boldly.

"I'm never gonna meet your parents or your brother, so you could tell me they have their own Satanic cult and they kill puppies for giggles, and I wouldn't know otherwise."

Hudson shifted his gaze to the table.

"But you haven't don't that. You haven't said anything terribly damning at all. Other than reminding me over and over, that you're a fuckup."

When he didn't answer, still, Tori took a deep breath.

"From where I'm sitting, I don't see a fuckup." She shrugged. "I see a fun guy who has some stuff on his mind."

CHAPTER 10

HUDSON

Either he was very cliché, or Tori was observant. She had nailed him in just a couple of hours with him. Hudson didn't hate anyone, but he often felt the hatred directed at him. Mostly from his parents, because Liam didn't think about him enough to hate him.

His parents didn't hate him.

He knew that.

But they loved him conditionally. He knew that, too.

"So." He cleared his throat. "Just so you know, I'm a mancala champion."

"Noted." She licked her lips as she set the game up.

"Why do you believe that but not that I like Elvis Costello?"

"I don't know." She looked up at him with a frown. "Why do I?"

"I used to play with my grandpa."

"That's very cool. Go first."

"Girls are always first," he argued.

Tori jerked her eyes to his and laughed. "Okay. Brownie points for that one, for sure."

Hudson took a drink and shook his head as he set his glass down.

"You're right," he said quietly, eyes on the board. "I don't hate them. I just wish they would allow me to be me."

He heard her soft little sigh, but he damned sure wasn't going to look at her now. As much as he wanted her understanding, her friendship, he didn't want her pity.

"I mean, they have one Liam. Why do they need me to be a carbon copy?"

From the corner of his eye, he saw her flinch and nod as she took her turn.

"I have friends who feel that way," she told him.

They played in silence for a few minutes, both sipping slowly on their beers.

"Have you been to the Basilica?" he asked her after a while.

"The Notre Dame Basilica?"

"Mmm." He nodded.

"Yeah."

"Did you go to mass there yesterday?"

"I did, actually. It's beautiful."

"There's a neat thing there in the evenings. A light and color show."

"Yeah? Have you done it?"

He sighed and nodded. "Yeah. I went a few weeks before Christmas."

Tori sat back and watched him as he contemplated the game board.

"By yourself?"

"Mmm." He nodded. He took his turn and then picked up his glass. "What?"

Tori shrugged. "I'm impressed as hell and sad for you at the same time."

"I don't want your pity."

"It's not pity," she argued. "I mean, we all have baggage, right? I don't pity you, but I can still feel for you. For what you're going through."

Hudson supposed she was right, but he still felt a little heartburn or something in his chest.

"So. What'd your dad have to say?"

"Mmm." She laughed. "Well, he told me hit the jackpot last night. He and his current lady friend are in Vegas."

"Nice."

"Says he bought Loni a necklace, but he's saving most of it."

"Wow. Must have been a nice jackpot."

"Maybe." She frowned over the game board. "On the other hand, he would get excited about winning a hundred bucks."

"Yeah, but then the necklace would have to have been a gum ball machine purchase."

Tori snorted and held her hand out over the table. Hudson lifted his for a high five. The touch of her skin on his was a firecracker sparking in his veins. Their eyes met and held for a moment, and then the moment was gone, and Hudson was left wondering if she felt anything.

"I haven't met this one."

"Would he ever remarry?"

"No." She shook her head, took her turn, and sat back to look at him. "He's too busy wining and dining all the pretty ladies. I really think he likes them all. He just doesn't want to be tied down."

"Liam doesn't want to be tied down," Hudson mumbled. "But I'm not sure he likes anyone."

"Dad's a good guy. Don't get me wrong," she said quietly. "He's a great dad. He just doesn't want to be married."

"Hey, if he treats you well, that's what matters."

"He does." She nodded. "And actually, now that they're divorced, he treats Mom well."

Hudson stared at her for a long, quiet moment.

"It's your turn."

He nodded. "I know. I'm just trying to picture your parents."

"I have pictures." She reached for her bag and pulled her phone out again. "Take your turn."

She scrolled through her pictures until she found something she apparently liked. Hudson took his turn with the mancala stones and then took her phone.

"That's my dad. Last summer."

The guy had longish, graying hair. But it was thick, wavy, probably what most women would call sexy. His warm blue eyes were lined with crinkles that Hudson assumed came from laughter, just from the way Tori talked about him. He was broad-chested and tall. Handsome, Hudson decided.

"He looks fun."

"Fun?" She snorted as she took her phone back. "He's a walking party, Hudson. Everyone loves him."

"Except your Aunt Faith."

"You listen." She nodded, impressed by his comment.

"Of course I do."

"This," she handed him her phone again, "is my mom."

Compared to her dad, Tori's mother looked very conservative and professional. She wore a pants suit, with a high-necked blouse under it. Navy and gray, the colors understated though not bland. Her reddish-brown hair fell away from her face in soft, short waves.

"She's pretty."

"She is," Tori agreed, "but don't tell her that. At least not until you compliment on her intelligence or organization or analytical thinking."

"Got it." He nodded as she took her phone back again. Rather than put it away, she set it on the table.

"Hudson?"

"Hmm?"

"It's still snowing."

CHAPTER 11

Tori

Tori paid their bill, and they bundled up to go back into the snowstorm. She still didn't love snow, but she didn't hate today nearly as much as she did a couple of hours ago. If Hudson was dressed for it—if she was dressed for it—she wouldn't mind building a snowman or even sled-riding. But her boots had a small heel on them, even if they were snow boots. And her jeans were dressy, and her wool coat was out of the question for fun in the snow. Besides, Hudson was wearing those tennis shoes. His toes might be purple by now.

Once they were ready for the cold, they stepped outside. Hudson took off, and though she assumed they were going to the Montreal Museum of Fine Arts, she wasn't sure. She realized she didn't care. Hudson could lead her to a grocery store or an office building, and she would enjoy it if they were together and talking.

When they arrived at the Museum of Fine Arts, he insisted on paying for her ticket. This time, though, they spent hours traipsing the halls, looking at, discussing the art. It was warm enough she shucked her coat quickly. Hudson insisted he carry it, even though she said it wasn't necessary. He was carrying her computer already.

She felt a bit ashamed of how she'd dismissed him so quickly earlier this morning, when he'd asked to borrow her charger. Though she still didn't love jogger pants, Tori had gotten to know Hudson, and she liked him. She was curious about his upbringing, about his parents. About his fuckups in Nashville, but she didn't feel the need to throttle him for information. If he sprinkled bits and pieces in on their day like salt, to make their conversation more interesting, fine. If he never told her the full truth, also fine. She liked him, and being with him was easy.

For a numbers person, he liked art. And he chatted about it with ease, as if he spent time studying methods and artists and history. Tori wasn't schooled in art, but she enjoyed visiting museums and galleries. She enjoyed strolling through this one, now, side by side with Hudson Jones.

He was cute.

When he wasn't watching, she eyed him closely, thinking a little trim on the beard and a change of clothes—including weather appropriate shoes—and he'd shine like a diamond.

Both of them were drawn to the Arts of One World and the Early to Modern International Art exhibits, though they wandered through everything, stopping often to study the sculptures and paintings. Hudson was much more relaxed, more into learning what everything was here than he had been with the illusions.

When they left the building, Tori's stomach rumbling, darkness crept in around the outside of the skies. The snow had slowed considerably, but as they walked, Tori could still see tiny flakes dancing on the wind.

"Still want to come to dinner?" Hudson asked her as they walked.

"Trying to get out of feeding me?"

"No."

"I want to come to dinner," she told him.

He still carried her computer bag, and he walked on the outside, closest to the street as if to protect her. Form what, she wasn't sure, but she didn't mind it. He was courteous without being obnoxious about it. She liked it.

"Can you draw?" he asked.

It was quiet out, as if the heaps of snow on the ground absorbed all sound. Only a few cars braved the streets, likewise, not many fool-hearted people were out walking tonight. Headlights and traffic lights lit the streets and surrounding buildings with color. Tori thought it was almost Christmas-like. Too bad she hadn't met Hudson before the holidays. A festiveness added to their already fun night would be nice.

Not to mention, maybe they would have found themselves under mistletoe at some point.

"Um." She looked up at him but quickly looked back at the sidewalk. It wasn't slick, and yet, who knew when her foot might come down on a slick spot? The last damned thing she wanted to do was spill all over the sidewalk or street in front of Hudson Jones. "No. Not even good with stick figures."

His snort drew her attention away from the walking path. Sure enough, her foot hit a slick spot. She wobbled, but Hudson threw his arm around her waist to steady her.

"You're okay," he assured her.

Funny. She was anything but okay. Jobless. Stuck in a foreign country and desperate to get home. In a quandary, a mini-life crisis, wondering what her life meant, what she should do now. But she felt oaky.

"Me neither," he agreed. "But I can draw dogs."

"I'm sorry?"

"I know. Weird. But I can draw dogs."

"Okay, sure."

"You don't believe me.."

"Not really."

"'kay. I'll show you. We need to cross the street here."

"You didn't show me a picture of your parents."

They stood shoulder to shoulder at the corner, waiting until it was safe to cross. She felt him shrug and looked up at him.

"I can, but they're nothing special," he promised her. "Or maybe they are, but they know it?"

"Did you have dogs? Growing up?"

"Did I what?"

"Dogs. Did you have dogs?"

"Oh." He steered her to a big glass door and into the entryway for an apartment complex. Tori tugged her beanie off and dropped her head back to look around. The place was very impressive. A lot of brass. The doors appeared to be solid wood rather than hollow plywood. The black marble floors shined as they crossed to the elevator. "Liam and I had a dog when we were six and four."

"And?"

"Actually, I guess he was Mom and Dad's dog. He was ancient. He hated two little boys wanting to play all the time. Pulling his tail. Disturbing his naps."

"Why do you draw dogs?"

He shrugged and drilled his finger into the up button for the elevator.

"I dunno," he said defensively. "I like them, I guess."

"Me too."

"What sort of business does your mom run?"

They elevator doors shrugged open, exposing a fancy, golden interior. They stepped into the car; Hudson punched the four button.

"It's a home design and décor place." She leaned on the back wall. "She started as an architect. Moved into home design. Did blueprints for a local builder for a while."

"That's kind of cool."

"It is," Tori agreed. "But she doesn't like that I went into education. I don't make any money."

"At least you don't have a real estate tycoon sister knockin' down the big bucks for her to compare you to."

"True." She nodded. "What are you fixing me for dinner?"

CHAPTER 12

HUDSON

He wasn't habitually clean or dirty. But Hudson was glad his place was in good shape as he unlocked his door and ushered Tori inside. This apartment was no smaller than his Nashville apartment had been at just under a thousand square feet. But most days, it felt tiny, soul crushing. Hudson knew it was simply because he didn't want to be here.

It was different, though, with Tori here.

It looked nice, trendy, like a spread from a magazine. The colors were all muted grays and cremes. All perfectly nice, all *beautiful* with Tori standing in front of the window, dipping her head just a bit to see outside. But the apartment was his parents' rental unit; it wasn't home. Hard to unpack and feel comfortable when your landlords hovered over you constantly, making sure you didn't breathe too hard and leave fog on the window.

"This is nice," Tori decided as she turned back to him. "Very modern."

Hudson laughed softly. "It is. Not my choice of décor at all. But the rent's not bad."

"Your parents own this place, don't they?"

"They do." He nodded. "Maybe, consider this my halfway house."

Tori watched him for a few moments and finally nodded. Hudson held his breath until she unbuttoned her coat and slipped it off. The beanie came next. Out of force of habit, Hudson reached for her things and hung them by the door. Tori slipped her boots off; her reindeer socks caught his eye.

"Nice socks."

With a soft chuckle, she wiggled her toes. "Thanks."

"So." He finally shrugged out of his coat and hung it by hers. "I can get you a glass of wine. I have nothing stronger here."

She nibbled on her lower lip for a second. Hudson kicked out of his tennis shoes. No hiding the fact that his socks were wet. He narrowed his eyes at her in warning as he pulled his socks off.

"Hmm. Look at that. Your feet are purple."

"Pretty sure I'll live," he told her.

"Wine's good."

"Okay. Make yourself at home. I'll be right back."

He left her to wander through the living room while he dried his feet off and found some ankle socks to pull on. Sitting on the end of the bed to tug them on, he noticed the legs of his joggers were wet, too. He glanced at his bedroom door, reached out to swing it mostly closed, and then found a pair of jeans so worn they were almost as comfortable as the joggers.

At least they might do a better job of keeping his dick hidden if it decided to wake up again.

Tori was standing at the window again when he returned to the living room. Then again, Hudson had no personal photos displayed. None of the art on the walls was his. What else was she going to look at? The place honestly had less life and color in it than if he were truly renting an apartment here from anyone but his parents.

She turned toward him when she heard him coming. Hudson wouldn't swear to it, but it seemed like surprise flashed in her eyes. Maybe admiration?

Right, Hudson, get over yourself.

"Okay. Wine?" He grinned.

"Yeah." She nodded.

Hudson ushered her into the kitchen and nodded to the island bar.

"Sit down."

"Thank you." She scooched onto the end stool and looked around as he snagged two glasses from the cabinet and took a bottle of cabernet sauvignon from the tiny little wine rack on his cabinet. It held six bottles; Hudson had two.

"You're thinking something," he told her as he worked the cork out of the bottle. Tori shot him a quick look, guilt written all over her face. "Tell me."

He poured two glasses, stuck the cork back in the bottle, and carried the glasses to the island. Their fingers brushed as he passed one to her. Hudson watched her eye their hands, like she felt the same spark of heat that he did.

"I just think..." She hesitated. Took a deep breath.

"That only a loser at this age lives where his parents tell him to live."

Chin tipped down, Tori laughed softly, sadly. She shook her head.

"That I look much better in denim than joggers."

She flicked her eyes up to meet his. "Yeah. But the joggers were growing on me."

Hudson threw his head back with a laugh. Hands still hovering close, their glasses close enough to clink, he itched to touch her again. Instead, he took a step back and lifted his wine for a drink.

"Tell me," he coaxed her. "Be brutally honest. I can take it."

She met his eyes finally, scraped her lower lip with her teeth, and took a quick breath. "I think it's sad that you live here. Like this."

"Under my parents' thumb."

"Yes and no," she mumbled.

"Explain." He spoke quietly, not offended but interested in her answer.

"I've known you for less than a day, and you're a very colorful, interesting person." She swept her gaze around the kitchen before meeting his eyes again. "This apartment is cold and dead."

Before Hudson could open his mouth, she held up her hand to stop him. "And yes, I get that it's because it's not *your* place. Maybe if you were renting some other apartment in the area with different owners, you might let some of your personality show. And maybe you're not doing it here out of spite."

If only spite worked with his parents.

"So," he sipped his wine and took a step back, "I can do steaks in a cast iron skillet. Or we can do salmon. Just shopped yesterday, so both are fresh."

"Salmon," she told him as he turned to the refrigerator. He set his glass down without looking and grabbed the door handle. "Are you angry? By what I said?"

"No," he answered honestly. "First of all, you're right."

CHAPTER 13

TORI

She watched Hudson as he grabbed a brown paper package from the fridge and set it on the counter. He wasn't looking at her, but he seemed at ease. His shoulders weren't tense; he moved fluidly, like he cooked often and maybe enjoyed it.

"What else?" she finally asked him.

"Elvis Costello," he reminded her with a glance. She answered with a smile. "Okay, so with the salmon, broccoli or bell peppers?"

"I don't want anything green in my teeth."

Hudson chuckled and squatted in front of an open cabinet. "Okay. Bell peppers it is." He pulled out two skillets and then straightened to put them on the counter. "Let me get some music going."

Tori nodded when he glanced at her on his way out of the room. She studied her wine, wondering what, if anything, this was leading to. No question she was attracted to him. Even with the beard needing a trim and the joggers he'd changed out of. Never mind how the denim fit him.

But it was more than that. More than physical. She liked him. He was fun. Charming. A little hard on himself, but she supposed he had reasons.

Did she want to know his reasons? Why he was a self-professed fuckup? What happened in Nashville, and why he let his parents dictate life choices to him?

Kind of.

But only because she saw through the tough guy veneer. He had issues with his parents, but he didn't hate them. He had mentioned little things, but he hadn't lingered over it. Rather than wallowing in any of it, he had taken her to the museums. They'd shared lunch and played a game.

The soft sounds of piano music filled the apartment. Tori wasn't familiar with Elvis Costello's music; she knew a song or two. But this sounded good, relaxing. Hudson returned to the kitchen and flashed her a boyish smile. Maybe the music was a little bit sexy. She closed her eyes and swayed a bit at the island as Hudson moved around the kitchen, clearly in his element.

"So, I'll pan sear the salmon," he told her. She opened her eyes to watch him, interested in the slide of his shoulder and back muscles under his t-shirt as he worked. "And then I'll stick it in the oven for a bit.

"You like this, don't you?"

He glanced at her as he pulled a cutting board from another cabinet and put it on the island counter by her. "I don't love this song as much as some of his others."

"Cooking."

Hudson stopped moving and looked at her with an arresting smile. Tori forgot to breathe.

"I do." He shrugged. "Although, it gets old cooking for one."

"Glad I could be of service."

His laughter trailed him back across the kitchen to the sink where he washed a couple of peppers and dried them. He carried them to the cutting board, went back to the counter for a knife, and returned, ready to get to work.

"Can I help with anything?" She would, but she didn't want to. Tori knew her way around a kitchen and could make herself useful. But she wanted to sit and watch him. She liked the way his lips curved just slightly while he worked. The way his unruly dark hair fell over his forehead when he looked down. The flex of his long fingers, his wiry forearms with a sparse covering of dark hair.

"Nope. You're doing great just right where you are."

"Okay."

She took a drink, deciding that he wasn't going to offer any other information or thought about her critique of his apartment. As interested as she was, she wouldn't pry. They'd had a good day. No need to ruin it now.

"I totaled my car," he announced as he chopped the first red pepper. "Drunk."

Tori wasn't aware of speaking, but she must have made some sort of noise, because Hudson flicked his gaze up for a moment to look at her.

"Twice."

"Wow."

He nodded at her whisper.

"Fortunately, no one was injured. I had some pretty bad bruises and cuts, but I didn't hurt anyone else."

"Good."

He wouldn't recover from that. No matter what she knew about Hudson Jones, she understood that the guilt, the regret, of hurting someone else would crush him.

"Yeah," he agreed. "The first time wasn't terrible."

She stared at him intently when he stopped chopping to look at her.

"I mean, drinking and driving is terrible. It's wrong, I know that. But the accident itself wasn't awful. Did enough damage that they had to total the car."

"How long ago was this?"

"Um." He raised his eyebrows. "Seven years."

She nodded.

"The second wreck was bad. I hit a tree." He cleared his throat. "Airbag saved my life, whether that's fortunate or unfortunate I haven't decided."

"Hudson." She covered his hand with hers, ignoring the little zap of electricity that shot through her.

"The thing is," he continued, "I don't drink all the time. I don't tie one on every night. I don't wake up hungover, desperate for a drink to kill the headache."

Eyes on her hand over his, she nodded for him to keep talking.

"I did have the tendency to drink more when I was younger. Sometimes the bottle felt like..."

"All you had."

"Cliché." He cleared his throat. "But there it is."

"Was the first accident in Nashville?"

"No. I was in Florida with friends. Second one was Nashville." He shifted a bit. Whether he was simply ready to begin chopping again or if he was uncomfortable with her touch, she didn't know. But she pulled her hand back and rested her forearms on the granite counter.

"Did you lose your license?"

"Second time I did."

"And when was that one?"

"Not quite a year ago."

He finished the first pepper and reached for the second one.

"Bad for the family name," he told her. "To have your younger son out drinking and totaling cars. Reflects badly on your older son. The superstar."

She bit her lip to keep from saying she was sorry. She was, of course she was. It galled her that parents treated children that way. But Hudson didn't want pity. That would probably be her ticket out of here, even before dinner was ready.

"But," he continued, "here's the thing. Liam went nuts two years ago. Got drunk and went after his girlfriend. Beat her up pretty bad. My parents paid her off. To keep her mouth shut. Because you know what would happen if the world knew the truth about Liam Jones."

"His soccer career would be over."

"Give the lady a prize," he mumbled.

"Why do you do what they want?"

"Well, I lost my job. Because of the accident. No license. No job. Couldn't pay my rent. So it was either be homeless in Nashville or live here and get back on my feet."

"Gotcha."

Hudson put the knife down and picked up his glass. He met her eyes as he took a drink.

"You can't possibly know how long I considered being homeless rather than come here."

The dark look on his face hurt. She wondered if he had ever been close to anyone. True to the man he'd been all day, he offered her a lopsided grin and carried the cutting board back across the kitchen. He was determined to play it off as if it were no big deal.

Tori lifted her eyes and looked around the kitchen wishing she had the words to heal him.

CHAPTER 14

HUDSON

Saying all of it out loud was weird. Well, he talked to his therapist, but he didn't count that. She couldn't be judgmental, or at least, she couldn't let it show if she did judge him. Tori could. She could be so disgusted with him right now that she could get up and walk out of his apartment, his life, and he would never see her again.

Wow. Earlier this morning, when he had asked to borrow her charger, he hadn't really even looked at her. She could have been an elderly grandmother type. She could have been a guy. Hudson just wanted a charger to escape the latest argument with his parents with the dumb game on his phone. Now, after hanging out with this woman for a few hours, he liked having her around. Her red curls and blue eyes were just icing on the cake.

Hudson felt a connection with Tori. He wanted the chance to explore it. Problem was, if things got out of hand—and he honestly had no idea if they were moving in that direction or not, and he was okay with either outcome—his dick might not cooperate. The last time he'd been with a woman, he'd been hard enough to start things, but damned if he could deliver. That had been so embarrassing, he hadn't even thought about sex in ages.

"Do you eat a lot of seafood?"

He glanced at her over his shoulder, relieved she had changed the subject. She probably read his body language. She was throwing him a rope here, because she knew if she said anything remotely supportive or comforting, it would smother him.

That was it. Right there. The connection. She knew what he was thinking and feeling. He had been close to his grandpa when he was a kid, but Hudson had never had that connection with anyone else. Not his parents. Not his brother. And never a girlfriend.

"I do." He nodded. "My favorite is branzino."

"Is he a musician or a designer?"

When he jerked his gaze back to hers, she was grinning.

"I know. It's fish," she said with a laugh. "I've never had it."

"Weirdest food you've ever eaten?" he asked as she slid off her stool and reached for her wine glass.

"Weirdest combo or just weirdest food?"

"You decide."

She moved up to stand beside him. "I've had fried anchovies. Which is weird for me."

"What're you doing?" He rested his hands on the counter and turned to look at her. Close enough to feel the heat from her body, to smell the rich, sweet scent of what he assumed was her perfume. "I got this."

"I know you do." She turned sideways at the counter and tipped her head at him. "But I don't want to talk to your back."

Hudson laughed softly when she leaned the opposite way to give his backside the once over.

"Not that I mind the view."

His dick decided that now was a good time to wake up. If only he could be sure the damned thing would stay alive long enough to do things right. Still, Hudson couldn't let the moment go without acknowledging what she'd said.

He twisted to face her, eyes locked with hers. She stared at him boldly, her wine glass still in her hand, resting on the counter. Hudson's heart slammed into his rib cage when those pretty blue eyes roamed lower over his face, his lips. If that didn't mean she wanted him to kiss her, Hudson had completely forgotten how to speak any language of love.

When she locked eyes with him again, he arched his eyebrow in question. Tori simply smiled. Careful, because today, because Tori, was fragile to him. Not Tori herself; nope, her strength, her feistiness, was part of what he liked about her. But what she might mean to him felt fragile, so new and so beautiful, he was afraid he would fuck things up yet again. Hudson lifted his right hand, the one that had held the knife, and just barely touched her. His fingers gently cupped her chin. Her soft, warm skin made his mouth go dry.

"What're we doing?" she whispered as she tipped her head toward him.

"I have no idea," he answered. "But I like it."

She laughed softly and scraped her teeth over her lip. "Me, too."

He wanted to dive in. To feast on her. To kiss and lick and touch every last inch of her body. But she was more than that. Tori Baker was more than a quick fling on the kitchen counter. More than any of that, Hudson wanted to sample. Her lips. The freckled skin over her cheekbone. The hollow between her shoulder and neck. He wanted to slide his fingers through her curls and watch her eyes slide closed in pleasure.

He had rushed through the past twenty-five years of his life looking for something to stop the pain. Maybe somewhere through the years he had learned it was the rushing, the charging through life, that numbed the sadness, the heartache he carried.

Maybe Tori was an angel in just the right place at just the right time to make him truly see himself. But maybe that was it—if Tori had appeared in his life for a reason, then Hudson was going to be the best version of himself for her.

They moved together, into each other. Their lips touched softly, warm and dry, and yet Hudson's heartbeat amped up like he was staring out the open door of a cargo plane, ready to jump. He smoothed his thumb over her skin and kissed her again. Still soft, still sweet.

She tipped her head back to look at him. And then just as before, they moved again, together, for another kiss. This time, Hudson parted his lips and waited, thrilling when he felt her warm breath on his face. He rubbed his lips over hers and flicked his tongue over the center of her lip—the same spot where she had just dragged her teeth. Tori's fingers climbed his arm and sank into his shoulder as their tongues brushed just slightly.

Hudson's dick was at full attention and part of him thought to strip her down and use it now before he lost his erection. He didn't want it to be that way. Not with her.

Instead, he pulled away and stepped back just enough to look at her. She dipped her chin to hide her small, shy, smile.

"Are you sure I can't help you with anything?"

CHAPTER 15

Tori

They'd moved on from Elvis Costello. Tori had no idea who was singing now, but the woman had a nice, smooth voice, and the music itself was jazzy and smooth. She loved it; she wouldn't have pegged Hudson for a jazz fan.

She had also loved the kissing and what it did to her body. She loved what it was still doing to her body. Sitting together at the island bar, over dinner and wine, her heart was still beating fast, and her belly fluttered with the wings of hope. Anticipation.

While she wasn't above a quick fling before returning home to her real life, before throwing herself into the job search and probably embracing a move or a career change, she wondered if this could be more. She and Hudson were young, both reasonably attractive, and single. This was natural. Being attracted to each other, considering a little intimate fun—natural. But something felt deeper, bigger.

"My dad took me golfing with him once," she told Hudson.

"You didn't like it?"

"It was more that Dad..." She pursed her lips and laughed at the memory. "Was not a golfer. And he was there to impress someone. And he kind of..."

"Belly-flopped?"

"Yeah." Tori nodded and pointed her fork at him. "That's a good way to put it. Needless to say, it didn't work out with the girl. And when I say girl, I mean girl. I think she was barely legal to drink."

"He didn't like the audience for his crash and burn?"

"Nope." Tori stabbed a piece of pepper and slipped her fork between her lips. Hudson knew how to cook. The peppers were flavorful; the salmon done just right. He'd added a bit of lemon and dill to the filets. Her belly was almost too full, too satisfied, to eat another bite. And yet, the thought of leaving anything to waste felt like a sin. "So. I just never went back."

"I used to kind of play with some friends, but none of us were good."

"That's kind of the best way to play sports, sometimes, isn't it?" she asked. "For fun?"

Their eyes met. Hudson's twinkled when he grinned. At times, Tori thought he looked sad. She loved his smile.

"It is," he agreed.

"Do you still play soccer?" She almost held her breath, afraid she was pushing him with her question.

"I haven't lately," he said quietly. "But I did when I was in Nashville."

"I like that."

Hudson tore his eyes away from hers and looked down at his empty plate. She finished off her salmon, set her fork down, and wiped her mouth with her napkin.

"Most of the time, it's fun," he told her. "But sometimes..."

"You can't always control the memories."

"The feelings the memories create."

She nodded. It occurred to her that his friends might have walked away from him after his accident. Drunk driving was a tough one. Unforgivable. Hudson had been lucky he hadn't seriously injured or killed anyone. But the idea of him having no one in his life made her heart hurt.

"Do you still talk to your friends there?"

"Most of them." He nodded. "And yes, they did read me the riot act. Well-deserved, I know. But um...yeah. We stay in touch."

"So, you're planning to go back to Nashville?"

Hudson pushed his plate away and picked up his glass. He was still sipping his first pour, while Tori was on her second. He swallowed the last of the wine and then studied the ring of red in the bottom of the glass.

"That's the plan."

She wondered why that hurt. It wasn't like it mattered to her if he stuck around Montreal. She would be going home when the snowstorm let up and she could get a flight.

"Ever been there?" He put his glass down.

"Nashville?" she asked and continued when he nodded, "Yes."

"Do you like it?"

"Yes."

He reached for her hand and linked their fingers. "You could visit me."

Would she, though? It was a wonderful thought. Right now. But what would happen when the snow stopped, and she boarded a plane to Illinois, and Hudson finally moved back to Nashville?

"I could."

Would he still want her to?

She cleared her throat and slipped off her stool.

"What're you doing?" he asked when she reached for his plate.

"You cooked. The least I can do is clear the table."

"You don't have to do that."

She ignored him and rinsed the plates before putting them in the dishwasher.

"Tell me something."

"Okay." He nodded when she looked back at him.

"When I look at you, I see like...blues music. Or hard rock."

"Is that a question?"

"But you like jazz?"

"Do you not like it? I can put on some Foreigner or Blue Oyster Cult."

"I love it, actually." She rested on the counter at her back. Hudson's smile lit the kitchen and finally, Tori thought it looked warm and inviting.

"So." She cleared her throat and looked around, afraid she would charge across the kitchen and climb into his lap. "What're you doing now? Here?"

"Working in an accountant's office."

"Except not today?"

He grinned. "It was a work from home day. Snow. Some of the employees couldn't do the commute with the snow."

"And this is working from home?" She looked around the kitchen again before looking at him.

"I was actually up at four, and I did what needed to be done."

"Eww. Why four?"

"I don't sleep a lot," he said simply. "Or I don't sleep when I should."

She could ask if he used sleeping aids, but again, that felt like poking a bit too far into his space. For now, she filed it away. At four a.m. this morning she had been curled up in her hotel bed sleeping like a baby. Still, it impressed her that he had done whatever work needed to be done already.

"Did you have to get rid of everything? When you moved?"

"Hmm?" Hudson stood and reached for her. Tori took his hand, heart racing again at his touch, at the wonder of what might come. "No. My stuff is in a storage unit. I refused to bring anything here with me. Because the minute I am secure enough to leave, I'm gone. This isn't home. I've never been home when I'm with them."

He slipped his arm around her waist and pressed his hand to the small of her back. Tori stepped into the living room.

"Okay, so if you decorated this apartment, tell me what it would look like," she said as he leaned in close behind her and pressed his cheek to her ear. He smelled clean and fresh; his warm skin a mix of soft and rough, where his beard touched her.

"Well," he started, "I would leave the color scheme. But I have a lot of posters."

"Concert posters or centerfolds?"

With his chest pressed to her, she felt his laugh rumble up her back.

"A few concert posters. Got rid of the centerfolds when I left college."

"Good."

"I have some cool artwork."

"I'm gonna guess abstract art. Not landscapes or fruit bowls."

"You are correct."

"Personal pictures?"

"Fishing again?"

"Well, I hope we're beyond that now." She tipped her head to look at him over her shoulder. "Pictures of friends? Vacations?"

"Yeah. I do have a lot of those. Some framed. Some would be stuck to my fridge with magnets. And some just tossed here and there."

"What're your friends like?"

"I think," he began as he stepped back and turned her in his arms, "you'll just need to visit me when I move back. And see for yourself."

"Yeah?" She looped her hands behind his neck and pressed her middle to his. His erection told her they were definitely on the same page.

"I don't want you to leave Montreal until I do," he said with a quick grin. "But at least promise me this isn't it. I want more than tonight with you, Tori."

"This isn't it," she whispered as he leaned in to kiss her again.

This was more than before, the kissing in the kitchen. Hudson still kissed her like she was precious; his mouth was soft and thrilling on hers. But his hands roamed her back now, smoothing over her hips and cupping her bottom. Tugging her closer.

"Tori."

His ragged whisper would have been enough to shatter things, but the way he suddenly pulled away from her left her cold and scared. The wings of hope, of anticipation, in her belly were now heavy with dread.

"What?" She shook her head. "What's wrong?"

Did he have a girlfriend? A wife? Was he just now going to come clean about it? She steeled herself for his excuse, for the reason behind his sudden change of heart. Maybe he just wasn't into her. Maybe—

"It's not you." He shook his head.

The gut reaction to strike out at him, to give him hell for leading her on or lying to her about being single, burned out when she saw the pain in his eyes. Rather than rail at him, rather than grab her things and run, Tori reached for him and stroked her fingertips down his arm. She felt his bicep bunch under her fingers as he lifted his hands to drag them through his hair.

"It's not you," he repeated.

"Tell me, Hudson," she whispered.

CHAPTER 16

HUDSON

Hands in his hair, he squeezed his head and turned away from Tori. He couldn't do it. He couldn't start this with her only to disappoint her. Disappoint himself again. But how the hell could he just blurt out the truth to her?

"Hudson." She spoke so calmly, he had to look at her. Dropping his hands, he put all his frustrations in a deep, long groan and met her eyes. "Do you not want to do this? Are we just going to be friends?"

"Fuuuck." He dropped his head back and squeezed his eyes closed.

"Hey. Listen."

He stiffened when she wrapped her fingers around his wrist.

"Listen to me."

Hudson gave in with a sigh and looked at her again. She gave his wrist a gentle squeeze.

"It's okay. Unless you tell me you have a wife or a girlfriend you forgot about, I'm not going anywhere."

"No wife or girlfriend," he said so quietly, he wasn't sure she heard him. "I promise you that."

"Okay." She nodded. The voice of reason. When he heard it from his mother, his therapist, he wanted to roll his eyes. Although, yes, when his mother spoke, judgment and disappointment far outweighed the reason. "Let's just be friends. I like you—"

"The last time." He snapped his teeth together so hard, pain shot through his jaw. "I'm on medication, Tori."

"Oh." She nodded. "Okay. I get it."

"You don't, though."

"Listen." She stepped closer to him, but she let go of his wrist. Hudson wanted to protest, to take her hand and wrap her fingers back around him. He liked the way it felt—both the slide of her warm skin on his and the feeling of compassion, of support. He breathed a deep sigh of relief when she rested her hands on his chest. "If you want to tell me, I'll listen. If you don't, it's okay."

"I want to do this, Tori." He cupped his hands around her neck and leaned in to rest his forehead against hers. "I'm just afraid..."

"I know." She nodded.

"I've been on it for years," he whispered, flinching at the pain. The words, the admission, was like glass in his throat, slicing him as he spoke. "Sometimes it's an issue. Lately, it's always an issue. But if I don't take it—"

"You have a lot going on," she reminded him. "A lot of stress. You're carrying a lot of guilt."

He huffed out another sigh. "I'm a thirty-two-year-old guy who can't get it up for a beautiful woman. That's a lot of stress right there...Liam and I both deal with it."

"Depression?"

He nodded. "The difference is he doesn't take anything. His lifestyle usually keeps him in check. The workouts. His diet."

"Okay." She slid her hands over his shoulders. "It's okay."

"He's not a bad guy." He lifted his head from her to look at her. "Well, I think he's a prick. But it's not like him to do what he did. To his girlfriend."

"And that worries you."

"Yeah." He shrugged. "It worries me that there's something seriously wrong, and my parents are pushing him to ignore it and focus on his career."

Tori simply rubbed her fingers over the back of his neck.

"God. I'm sorry." He shook his head and stepped back from her. "I'm so sorry. I shouldn't have dumped this. I should never have bothered you this morning—"

"I hope you don't mean that." She did that thing again with her teeth on her lip. His heart, his gut, his dick—everything raced in reaction. "Just because we don't have sex doesn't mean there's nothing worth exploring between us."

He scrubbed his hands down his face and backed away further. "I know. And I agree. I'm just...I'm angry. I'm embarrassed. I'm—"

"Hudson."

"What?"

"Do you want me to go?"

"No."

"Good." She nodded and reached for him again. "Because I really like the way you kiss me."

"Are you sure?" He slipped his hand in hers and rubbed his thumb over the back of her hand.

"Yes."

She met him halfway, her parted lips meeting his as he moved toward her. Tori inched her hands up his arms, as if she was afraid to spook him. Either that or maybe she, like he did, wanted to savor every touch. Their tongues slid together in a sensual dance. Hudson felt his heart beating everywhere in his body, everywhere all at once. His dick was wide awake and hungry for all of her, but that dark, ugly fear hovered over Hudson like a vicious storm.

He sculpted his hands over her hips and sank his fingers into her butt to get a firm grip. The soft mewl in her throat was like a snort of cocaine, a jolt of raw electricity on the tip of his dick. Before he realized he was moving, he tugged at her shirt, his fingers hungry for the heat of her skin.

Tori stepped back just enough to lift her shirt and tug it over her head. The lavender lace bra that offered her breasts in a sweet, pretty little package took his breath away. He opened his mouth, ready to ask, to beg, but before he could speak, she reached back and unhooked it.

Hudson tugged the straps gently, admiring the feel of her skin under his fingers, the slow revealing of her bare breasts, as he pulled the lace away.

"You're sure?" He stopped himself before touching her.

"Yes."

"Even if I can't—"

"I like the way you kiss me," she said again. Hudson swallowed hard when he realized what she meant, what she wanted. Entirely possible that he might just come in his jeans before he got his mouth on her. He wasn't sure if that was any better than his recent problem.

"C'mere." He moved again, slid his arms around her, and cupped her butt again. Reading his mind, maybe as desperate for what came next as he was, Tori wrapped her legs around his waist when he lifted her. She leaned into him, her breasts pressed to his chest, and nibbled her way from the hollow in his shoulder to his neck, just under his ear.

"I feel your heartbeat," she whispered. "On my lips."

He carried her to his bedroom and eased her gently to his bed. Tori, on her back, scooched up a bit on the unmade bed. Her pale skin, the rosy peaks of her breasts, looked delicious on his dark gray sheets. She propped herself on her elbows and watched him tug his own shirt over his head. He hesitated, hands near his zipper. His dick was about to explode out of his jeans right now, but who the fuck knew how long that would last?

Eyes locked with his, she licked her lips.

"It's up to you."

From the corner of his eyes, he saw her fist his sheets in her hands. Turned on by the image, the thought of her hands on his dick, he unbuttoned his jeans. She offered him a slow, sexy smile when he tugged the zipper down.

"The joggers did grow on me," she said, still wearing that same smile, "but there's nothing sexier than a man unzipping his pants, getting ready for his woman."

Crazy, irrational hope roared through him like wildfire. It was early, much too soon to think of Tori Baker as his woman. For her to consider herself his woman. But fuck if he didn't want that now.

"Maybe one thing," he corrected her. She arched her brows as she watched him kick out of his jeans. She eyed his dick, still bulging behind his boxer briefs, but she eyed everything else, too. His hair, his beard, his shoulders. Opting to leave his underwear on for now, he stalked toward her and pressed a knee to his mattress.

"What one thing?" She sounded out of breath.

He didn't answer. Instead, he unzipped her jeans and eased them inch by inch over her hips when she lifted them. He tugged them down over her knees, lower still, and finally dropped them on the floor. Her thong was the same color as the bra they'd left on the living room floor. The lace a mix of sultry and sweet, feminine. Hudson brushed the back of his hands down her inner thighs, delighting when she parted her legs wide for him.

"This might be the sexiest thing, ever." He brushed his thumb down her center, loving the sensation of lace and wet heat on his skin.

Tori, apparently tired of waiting, sat up further and reached for him. She wrapped an arm around his neck and tugged him closer, putting her parted lips on his face, missing his lips altogether.

"I think the sexiest thing about you is the way you kiss." She tugged at him and then tumbled him onto the bed with her. The feel of her warm breasts on his chest made him forget to breathe. Again, he fought the rush of desire, the need to grab her everywhere and squeeze and rub and end everything before it started.

In his slight hesitation, Tori gave his shoulder a gentle push. He fell to his back and nearly cried out in pleasure when she climbed over him to straddle his hips. She rolled her hips just once, dragged her heat over his dick, and then leaned forward to kiss him again.

She swept her tongue deep inside his mouth, exploring, touching, pleasuring him as much as she claimed he did her. Her curls were a soft curtain around his face; her hands roaming over him as she kissed him. One hand moved over his face, his neck, his shoulder, and the other, she tangled in his hair.

Hudson stroked his fingers up his sides, laughing when she wiggled and squealed a bit. But she moaned with pure bliss when he cupped her breasts and brushed his thumbs over her nipples. He wanted her higher, her breasts in his face, in his mouth, but he wouldn't release her to move her. As if she read his mind, as if she wanted his mouth on her, she scooted up over him, her wet heat now over his stomach, and offered herself to him.

CHAPTER 17

Tori

He latched onto her nipple firmly and tugged with a hard, delicious sucking motion. Tori gasped at the pleasure that rippled through her. He played there with his lips and his tongue for what felt like forever and like a second before moving to treat her other nipple in the same way. Tori rubbed over Hudson's stomach, the beginnings of an orgasm teasing, lapping at her.

"Let me do that." He flipped her so that she was lying under him on the bed. Tori closed her fingers around the back of his head and pulled him in to kiss him again. His beard scratched her face, her lips, and then her neck. When he dipped his head to her breasts to play again, she threw her head back and dug her heels into the mattress. Hudson smoothed his hand down her belly and slipped his fingers inside her thong.

She moved with him, riding his hand as he teased her with short, quick strokes and deeper, longer strokes. Tori panted, struggling to catch her breath, her fingers in his hair again. The orgasm climbed over her a bit at a time, coming hard and fast and then falling away when he eased the pressure on her core.

"Please, Hudson," she whispered.

"I want to be inside you." He flicked her nipple with the tip of her tongue.

"Please. Do it harder." She pulled at his hair. "I'm so close."

He pressed harder on her core and slid a finger inside her as he bit down on her nipple. Tori shattered and squeezed her eyes closed as she screamed his name. Before she fell from the clouds, he scooched back over her belly and hooked his fingers in her panties to slide them off. She drew her knees up as Hudson kissed a trail down her inner thigh.

She came again in minutes, and frozen with pleasure, she watched the stars play on the ceiling in his room.

"You okay?" His gruff voice stirred her from her musings. She laughed softly and lifted her head to look at him, still poised between her legs.

"You made me see stars."

"Sounds like a good thing." He arched an eyebrow. "What about moonlight? See any of that?"

"Not yet, but I'd like to."

He laughed when she wagged her eyebrows.

"I don't mean to pressure you," she said sincerely. "It's okay if you don't—"

"I wanna make love to you," he assured her. "It's just...really fuckin' awful when you're in that...position...and..."

"The fishing pole breaks?"

"It doesn't even break." He huffed a laugh as he scooted off her and stood at the side of the bed. "It just goes limp. Kinda hard to impress you with a soft dick."

"Hudson." She shook her head. "I wouldn't be here with you if you hadn't impressed me earlier today."

"Yeah?" He grinned. "What did it? The joggers? Or the beard in desperate need of a trim?"

"Your smile," she answered simply. "Your offer to hang out with a tourist stranded in a snowstorm."

She watched with wide eyes when he pushed his boxer briefs down and his cock sprung free. Long and thick, it arched toward her, like a dog straining at its leash.

"Do you want me to..." She stopped talking when he stretched over the bed toward the nightstand. His thighs were warm on her belly, his hard cock pressed into her breast. Tori turned her head to see him pull a box of condoms from the drawer. She lifted her head and flicked her tongue over his head.

"God." He arched into her but caught her chin in his hand. "As good as that feels, I want my dick inside you. I wanna move in you. With you."

"Me, too." She nodded and waited patiently for him to open the wrapper and pull the condom out. He hesitated, on his knees, cock jutting toward her. She caught herself before she could assure him again that it was okay, no matter what happened. As much as she meant it, maybe that wasn't the right thing to say to motivate him. "Love me, Hudson."

She said it that way on purpose. Because she felt connected to him. Whatever he did to her right now, what he had already done to her—it was all good. He lifted his chin and met her eyes as he rolled the rubber on. Tori reached for him, moaning with sheer longing when he stretched out over her, and drove into her hard and fast, as if he was afraid he would miss his chance.

Legs wrapped around his waist, she moved with him. She arched her back and met him thrust for thrust. He was hard and deep inside her, filling her, touching all the spots she needed him to touch. Best of all, he kissed her. Long, deep kisses. Short and sweet kisses. Tongues and lips and teeth, stroking, licking, biting. He kissed her until at last, she couldn't breathe for the waves of pleasure that rolled over her and drowned her. Even when she was no more than a boneless puddle of pleasure under him, she squeezed her thighs around him and worked him hard, thrilling when she felt him stiffen over her. He ducked his head to rest on her shoulder, his ragged breath tickling her neck, her ear.

THE SULTRY jazzy music drifted down the hall from the living room. Tori moaned her satisfaction as Hudson stroked his fingertips up and down her back. She lay on her stomach, her arms stacked under his pillow. Hudson—having kissed every inch of her skin from the tips of her toes up to her hairline and then playing with her hair, kissing her head, too— lay at her side, one leg thrown over her, his knee pushing gently into her butt when he moved.

"I don't wanna leave," she said quietly.

"Stay."

"I meant ever."

He laughed softly and leaned close to drop a kiss on her shoulder.

"Stay as long as you want," he suggested. "You make this place a hell of a lot brighter and warmer than anything I could ever bring in here."

"Bet you say that to all the girls." She lifted her head and turned to look at him.

"I think we've established that there haven't been many girls for a long while."

Tori twisted around until she was lying on her back and looking up at him.

"When you were drinking...the second time you wrecked your car."

He nodded, though he avoided her eyes.

"You said you hit a tree."

"I did."

"Was it..." She held her breath, unable to say it. Had he done it on purpose? Had it been more of a suicide attempt than a drink driving accident?

"I dunno." He swallowed hard. Tori's eyes were drawn to his Adam's apple. She lifted her hand and stroked her fingers down his throat. "Maybe. I guess. I don't know."

"Is that maybe why?" She hesitated again. "Your parents wanted you here? Maybe it's the only way they can show you they love you?"

CHAPTER 18

HUDSON

"Helluva way to show your love."

"I didn't say it was the right way." Tori stretched, her body long and lithe against him, like a cat. His dick had survived making love to her; in fact, as far as he could tell, she'd enjoyed the fuck out of it, same as he did. But it was dead now. Most of the time, that kind of stretch, that purring and the light scrape of a woman's toenails down his leg, would wind him back up, and he'd be balls deep in her again in two seconds flat.

"I s'pose," he grumbled. "But playing second string son gets old. Especially when their perfect child isn't any more perfect than I am."

"Do you ever talk to them about it?"

"No." He ground his teeth together to keep his mouth shut. Tori was just trying to help. No need to fly off the handle at her for feelings he kept locked up for his family.

She trailed her hand down his chest, her fingers fanning out over his hips.

"What do you serve for breakfast?"

He laughed when she looked up at him.

"English muffins and eggs."

"No sausage?"

"We could try that." He met her eyes with a small smile.

"What happens when I leave?"

"We exchange numbers."

"And what? We talk on the phone like BFFs?"

"What do you want to happen?" He pushed her curls away from her face.

"I don't know. But I do know I'll want to see you again."

"Well, I can't drive, but I can fly."

"You need to save your money," she argued softly. "So you can get out of here and back to your life."

He hooked his arm around her and smoothed his fingers down her side.

"True. But I would like to have you in that life."

"Tell me about your friends there."

He sighed and shrugged, shifting the pillow under him slightly. "They're good people. I have a few friends from the office. A few I met in a soccer league."

"Pro—"

"Recreational," he cut her off. "Umm...You know how it is. You meet people. You meet more people through those people. Some are okay. And some you click with."

They shared a smile.

"Did they take you to the hospital? When you hit the tree?"

Eyes back on the ceiling, he nodded.

"Did your friends show up for you?"

"Three of them did."

Tori moved her hand from his hip to his face. She smoothed her thumb over his lips. "Good."

"I got lucky." His voice was heavy with anger. "And I don't mean because I lived or because I had someone waiting to take me home."

"I know." She nodded.

"I don't take that lightly."

"I get that, but I also think you need to forgive yourself."

"It was stupid. *I* was stupid."

"Agreed." She scooted up the bed a bit to kiss his cheek. "But I don't think you would do it again."

"What makes you think that? It was my second strike."

"I think you learned your lesson."

"What about you?"

"What?"

"Ever wrap your car around a tree?"

"No, but I rear ended a city bus once."

"Ouch."

"Ouch for my car."

"Biggest mistake you ever made."

"Mm." She rested her forehead on his cheek and closed her eyes. "Toss up."

"Between?"

"Losing my virginity to a guy who was six years older than me."

"How old were you?"

"Eighteen."

"Did he hurt you?"

"No, but it wasn't all stars and moonlight, either."

"Isn't that pretty standard for girls?"

She lifted her head and smirked at him.

"What else?" He lifted his other hand and tweaked her nipple.

Tori scrunched her nose up like something smelled rotten.

"I slept with one of my dad's friends."

"Ooh. Ouch. That." Hudson nodded. "Does your dad know?"

"Well, I sure didn't tell him." She rolled her eyes.

"Why would you do that? Is he like your dad? Is he married?"

"I don't know. Yes. And no."

"You're kidding, right? You owe me more than that."

"The guy I had been seeing for two years had just dumped me. Got a promotion at his law firm. And told me he didn't want a family, and if he only wanted a woman for sex, he wanted someone better than me"

"Damn." Hudson flinched. "For the record, I can't imagine he ever found that."

She arched her eyebrows. "You're only as good as your company or partner, right?"

He grinned and brushed her hair back again.

"So, I went to the bar. My girlfriends were all busy. So I went alone. I knew the bartender, so I knew I had a safe way home. I'd been there about an hour when Marty showed up."

"And he asked what was wrong, flattered you, bought you drinks, and fucked you."

"Yes. Yes. Yes. And yes."

"How was it?"

"Pretty incredible, really," she answered. "But it was just one night. And then I had to face my dad. And I know Marty's ex-wife. His kids. So it just felt wrong. Hard to be around him even now."

"Yeah, okay, so I would vote that sleeping with your dad's friend is probably worse than when you lost your virginity."

She dipped her chin, but not before he saw her lopsided grin. "Yeah. I think you're right."

"Do you like country music?"

"Sure."

"Lot of that in Nashville."

"You don't say." She chased her laughter, dipping close to kiss his neck.

"Where will you look for work?"

"I don't know." She shook her head. "I have the feeling I won't be a literacy reading specialist anymore. Not when there's not even enough funding for classroom teachers."

"What would you do then?"

She sighed. "I can teach. Because that's obviously a good choice with education budget cuts. Guess I can flip burgers."

"You can flip my burger anytime."

"My dad invited me to come out and stay with him for a week."

"Weird transition." Hudson squeezed his eyes closed.

"Maybe. But he would like you."

He snorted. "Sure. He'd want all the details about the things I did with his daughter."

"No, but he'd take you shopping. Get you some crazy deal on work wear or clubbing attire."

"I don't club. Not anymore."

"Good." She pressed her thumb over his lips again. 'That was a test."

"Very teachery of you. Giving me a pop quiz."

"I'd give you a gold star if I had one."

"Where would you put it?"

She quirked an eyebrow at him. "You really wanna know?"

"The dick with the gold star." He nodded. "Sounds like one of those little books but for chicks instead of kids."

"I'd buy it." She shrugged. "I was thinkin' more along the lines of the big cock that—"

"Don't you dare!" He laughed as he pushed her over on her back again. Hudson loved the thrill in her screech as he grabbed her sides to tickle her. "I think this dick's ready to do you again."

CHAPTER 19

TORI

They drank their coffee in bed the next morning. While she showered, he fixed her breakfast. She sat close to him in a pair of his joggers and his t-shirt while they ate scrambled eggs and English muffins. He kissed her neck and played with her hair while she cleaned the kitchen up. Tori didn't want the magic to end, but it was Tuesday, and the snow had stopped. And now, she had to navigate the several feet of snow on the ground back to her hotel and pack up again. She wouldn't get an immediate flight, but she had to book something. Time to go back to real life.

Hudson had to work, too. He had already answered three phone calls since they'd awoke in each other's arms earlier. While she hated the interruption, Tori liked the opportunity to observe his professionalism. He had it in spades, the same as he did charm and sex appeal.

"What're you doing?" she asked when he sat down in the kitchen to put snow boots on.

"Walking you to the hotel."

"What?" She shook her head. "No. I'll be fine."

"I am one thousand percent sure you will always be fine and able to take care of yourself," he said with an easy shrug. "But I want to spend a few more minutes with you. We spent the night together. I don't want that to be our last thing."

"What do you mean?"

He tugged on his other boot and stood. In a different pair of jeans, a flannel button-up shirt, and a beanie, he almost looked like a different man today. But his smile was still hers; she still got a little lightheaded when he aimed at her.

"Last night was so good, I want to do it again and again and again." He took her face in his hands and kissed the tip of her nose. "And while I want you in Illinois remembering what it felt like with me inside you, I also want you to remember there's more. To whatever it is we found together."

"Wow." She cleared her throat. "You're pretty sweet."

"When I want to be," he said with a nod; "and I am sweet on you."

"Where were those boots yesterday?"

"Say what you want, but me changing into the jeans and putting on dry socks last night is what really turned you on and got you in my bed."

"Right." She nodded, kissing him and laughing at the same time.

The snow might have stopped, but the temperature hadn't climbed a bit. Outside, they walked in frigid air the several blocks that took them from his apartment to her hotel.

"I have an idea," he told her when they stepped into the lobby.

"Not here."

He chuckled as he linked their fingers.

"There's a lot here we didn't get to do together."

"I think we made a deliberate choice to do what we did."

"Sssh." He grinned and tapped his finger to her lips. "I would love to do the AURA Experience at the Notre Dame Basilica."

"I kind of felt like I saw the northern lights last night. Is it anything like that?"

Hudson let go of her hands and took her by the shoulders. "And we could play in the snow on Mount Royal."

"Hmm." She frowned. "How is that even tempting when I hate snow?"

"You might hate snow, but you kind of like me."

"Give the gentleman a prize." She met his eyes. "You want me to come back for a visit?"

"I want you to come here. I'll hitch hike to you." He shrugged. "Whatever it takes, I just want to see you again."

"I want that, too."

"Okay." He nodded.

"Go now, before I get weepy. It's gross. This is bad enough." She swept her hand down indicating her natural face, messy hair, and his baggy clothes she had borrowed.

"You're beautiful," he told her.

Tori met his kiss with parted lips. She kissed him back with all the emotions she couldn't understand, let alone speak. They'd had a fun night, but her life beckoned. His job wouldn't wait, and his job was important if he wanted to get out of Montreal and back to his *life*. She hoped they would stay in contact, but she wasn't naïve. Just because they both claimed to want more didn't mean it would happen.

"Thanks for the best walking tour I've ever had." She brushed her fingers over his face.

"Of Montreal or anywhere?" He quirked an eyebrow at her.

"Anywhere."

He nodded and stepped back. "Let me know when you get to the airport."

"I will."

He hesitated again, for just a second. Tori held her breath until he turned and walked back outside. She watched his shoulders lift and then droop under his coat as if he had sighed. He tucked his hands in his pockets and walked away without another look back.

CHAPTER 20

HUDSON

He walked straight back to his apartment. Montreal wasn't his first choice of cities to live in, but it had nothing to do with the cold. Hudson hardly noticed the brisk wind or the snow piled on the sidewalks. Today, though, he wasn't thinking about his life in Nashville, the one he wanted to get back to. He was thinking about Tori, hoping their promises to stay in touch weren't the empty kind that people made just for something to say.

Once home, though he was reluctant to call his apartment home—and yes, Tori was right; part of his refusal to make himself at home here was simply spite—he forced himself to walk past his bedroom and get in the shower, rather than climb back into bed and curl up in the sheets, on the pillow that smelled like Tori. The office was open today, but even if it weren't, he would go in. Nothing good would come of hanging out here alone.

They had swapped numbers, of course. And Hudson wanted to call her or text her—something. But he waited. The ball was in her court at the moment; he had walked her back to her hotel. It hadn't been a gesture, something to impress her. He'd done it because he wanted to be with her a few minutes longer. And what he had said to her about not wanting sex to be their last thing together was true. Kind of felt like a pussy for saying that, but on the other hand, he had never put himself out there like that, gotten emotionally naked for a woman.

Maybe that was why he was still single. He liked Tori. If slapping his heart on his sleeve was a way to her heart, he was okay with the risk.

Dressed in flat front khakis, a button-down shirt, and a wool coat, he left the apartment, still thinking about Tori. Even after being inside her, spending the night with his skin pressed against hers, he kept coming back to her at the coffee shop. That slightly wicked look in her eyes when she told him she wasn't offering to get him a refill. The way she'd stopped just inside the pub to revel in the heat. In his memories, he wasn't just hearing her soft mewling sounds and the way she screamed his name when he made her come. It was her laughter—sometimes soft and sweet, sometimes sharp and sarcastic, and sometimes big and bawdy.

His phone rang as he walked to the office. He pulled it from his pocket, hoping it was Tori. And yet, if it were one of his parents, he would answer and deal with it. Tori had reminded him that hiding from his parents wasn't a good way to get through this miserable little slice of his life. In fact, their ultimatum about moving here and getting his act together might not have been entirely selfish. Sure, they wanted to protect the family name and protect Liam. But maybe they wanted to help him. After all, they could have let him rot in Nashville. He could be couch surfing at friends' houses. Hudson had good friends, but how long would they put up with that? He could be living on the streets in Nashville, and Hudson knew that was a slippery slope. Pretty hard to clean up and find a new job if he was sleeping on park benches and splashing water on his face in a public restroom and calling it a shower.

Tori's blue eyes shined at him from his phone screen. He'd taken a picture of her to put with her contact information. When she tried to take his picture, he had balked, told her no. But in true Tori Baker fashion, she had wrestled him and climbed on top of him on the couch. After a few playful kisses, he'd given in.

"Hey."

"Hi." She sounded chipper. He wasn't sure what to make of that. Happy to get the trip home in motion? Sure. Happy to get away from him? God, he hoped not. "What're you doing?"

"Walking to work," he answered. "You?"

"At the airport." She yawned. "Flight's not for another couple of hours, but at least I got one booked."

"Another couple of hours we could have been together."

"Mmm." She sounded wistful. Hudson could imagine the look on her face right now. "I know. But you need to work."

"I know."

"I talked to my dad again. I might go out there."

"Yeah?"

"I mean, I'm gonna go home first. Work on some job research. But. It's not like I don't have the time to go visit him."

Hudson side-stepped a couple walking at him hard and fast. He looked over his shoulder at them and then turned his attention back to her.

"You should. Soak up some warm weather."

He wanted her to go. It would be good for her. Seeing her dad and enjoying some warmer weather. But he hated that if she were going somewhere, she wasn't coming here.

"I wish you could go with me."

"Really?"

"Yeah. Imagine the trouble we could get into there."

"I like the sound of that," he said with a laugh. "So, what do you do on the plane?"

"Fly?"

"No. I mean you, specifically. Are you a reader? Do you work? Watch movies on your iPad?"

"Oh." She giggled. "Well, I work most of the time, but that involves reading."

"Like what?"

"I read a lot of kids' books. Do lesson plans. You know, to work on vocabulary and spelling and comprehension."

"It almost sounds fun."

"It is," she said quietly. "I guess today I can just read something for myself."

"I'm guessing you read thrillers."

"I do. What are you wearing?"

"Tori Baker, I am walking in public. Not to mention it's frigid cold out here. We are not having phone sex right now."

She answered him with that big, bawdy laugh. "Now you're getting me in trouble. An elderly couple is giving me dirty looks like we really are doing that."

"I didn't start it!"

"I meant do you wear joggers to work?"

"Oh." His turn to laugh. "No. I'm dressed like an actual adult today."

"Ooh. I wanna see."

"What?"

"Send me a picture."

"I'm bundled up in a wool coat right now. You want me to unbutton and risk frostbite?"

"Ha! You weren't worried about that yesterday."

"Again. My sexy feet got you in my bed."

"Ohmygod." That laugh again. Hudson felt a pang of loneliness already. "When you get to work, slip into the bathroom or a coatroom or something and take a selfie."

"Are you serious?"

"Dead serious."

"I feel like we're fourteen."

"Thank God, we're not. It would be pretty damned hard to see each other again if we were just kids."

Hudson took a deep, silent breath. That pang of loneliness spread through him and settled into something softer, warmer. She wanted to see him again.

"I'll show you mine if you show me yours."

Tori cracked up again. Hudson wondered what the elderly couple watching her was thinking. How could they not be charmed by that laughter? By her bright blue eyes.

"Okay. Sure."

He looked up as he crossed the street in front of his building. "I gotta go. Text me? When you get on the plane?"

"Will do. Bye, Hudson."

CHAPTER 21

TORI

She did a double take when Hudson sent his picture. And then she spent the first several minutes of her flight just looking it. Remembering. He was right—remembering their night together was nice, but it was even better to think about their little tour of Montreal and their lunch at the pub and the fact that he wanted to walk her to her hotel this morning. Good thing she'd asked for a late checkout. She would hate to be charged for another night on top of having the room and not using it.

Then again, it had been worth it.

The lighting wasn't great, and the background made the picture less than perfect for framing. He was in a coat room of some sort, but there was a mirror, so she was looking at a full-length picture. Hudson looked delectable in the flat front khakis and light blue button-down shirt. The tennis shoes were gone; he wore brown loafers. No better for the snow, but they looked good. He had trimmed his beard, too. Tori brushed her fingers over his face in the picture wishing she could kiss him again.

Finally, figuring she was creeping the guy out who sat next to her, she put her phone away and opened the book she'd packed. She didn't read, though. Instead, she stared out her window thinking about what came next. She would get home. Probably clean her place, just because it would help her get her head on straight. Decide if she was interested in a career change or a change of location. Or both. Whatever it took. She hated not working, both because she was a busy body and needed to do things and because she liked her job, she liked the kids she worked with.

She had called her mom after talking to Hudson. True to form, her mom had sounded happy to hear from her, but busy. Always busy. Tori didn't tell her about Hudson. That was too new; she wanted to keep that special and quiet for now. She did tell her she was considering going to visit her dad. As she assumed she would, her mom encouraged her to go. It would be fun. As different as their family was, she loved her parents and enjoyed being with them. She didn't even mind her dad's girlfriends that much. But now, after meeting Hudson and having to leave Montreal, she didn't care to see any hand-holding or worse.

She had sent him a selfie, though she didn't want to. Dressed in an oversized sweatshirt and leggings, she felt like a bum. To make it worse, she'd pulled her curls back in a messy bun and skipped the makeup. Hudson had responded and told her she looked adorable.

How long would it take him to get back on his feet and move back to Nashville? It wasn't a daytrip, but it was drivable. But again, maybe she was jumping the gun. No need to worry about it now. She finally focused on her book to pass the rest of the time on her flight.

* * *

IT WAS cold in Illinois but not like Montreal. She blasted her heater on the drive from the airport to her apartment. Turned the radio on and sang along to a Daughtry song, but she wished it was Elvis Costello. Might be warmer in Illinois, but Montreal had Hudson. She missed him already.

She spent the rest of the week cleaning. Even when she was exhausted, she dug through her dresser drawers and her closets and tossed things she hadn't worn in ages. She scrubbed her bathroom and the floors. Cleaned the oven and the refrigerator. And finally, when there was nothing left to scrub, she found herself at her computer, looking for job openings.

Every day, she and Hudson texted, whether it was a real catch-up text or just silly memes or jokes. Every night, when she crawled into bed, they talked on the phone. She had called him first. He called next. From there, she lost track. He told her he was cooking more again and searching for jobs in Nashville. Jobs and a place to live. Tori had no idea what sort of savings he had, what sort of agreement he had with his parents. She didn't have any experience with drunk driving charges, either. While she knew Hudson had lost his license, she didn't know if that was an automatic black strike on him when he was looking for work. And yet, his plans, the fact that he was thinking, looking for things now, made her wistful.

Her life was at a crossroads now, and if Hudson was making life changes, she hoped to be a part of his life. Much too soon to consider living together but not to think about living closer to each other. She didn't necessarily need to live in Nashville, but she could look for a job in that area.

She couldn't plan on that, though. Not yet. So, when she found a teaching position open in her area, she applied. She applied for a literacy coach position at a college within driving distance. And she found a couple of freelance editing jobs for the meantime.

Then she booked a flight to visit her dad. Even seeing him having fun with a girlfriend would be better than sitting alone in her apartment with nothing to do.

CHAPTER 22

TORI

From the corner of her eye, she saw her dad tip the bottle of cabernet sauvignon over her glass to refill it. She didn't need it; since she'd been out of work, she'd done a lot of sitting around and eating and drinking. Not a good thing for her figure. Although, Hudson had just told her last night on the phone that he liked her figure—among other things. Cheeks burning, she kept her eyes on her laptop screen when her dad sat down at the patio table with hr.

"This is so much better than the weather in Montreal," she told him without looking at him. It wasn't blazing hot, but she was perfectly comfortable in a pair of skinny jeans and lightweight three-quarter length sleeve shirt.

"You always did hate snow." He stared at her long enough that she had to meet his gaze.

"Maybe because you and Mom didn't take me out in it much when I was a kid. I don't get the fun of being outside in snow. When I could be inside with a book or a movie."

Or Hudson.

"That was our mistake," he told her with a nod. "We made a lot of mistakes, Tori."

"Nah." She shook her head as she reached for her glass. "You didn't, Dad. Maybe the snow thing was a mistake, but you and Mom were the best parents I could have asked for."

"The only parents you were going to get."

She laughed softly. Maybe so, but she had been reminded that she was blessed to have them when Hudson told her about his parents. Even if they did love him in their own way, she much preferred her own dysfunctional family.

"You should learn to ski."

"I've never even been sledding riding," she reminded him.

"Go big or go home." He shrugged.

"Speaking of going big, Aunt Faith is thinking about moving to Amsterdam."

"Oh." Her dad looked shocked. "Does your mom know that?"

"Yeah, they've been talking about it."

"Well, okay." He grinned. "Think big like Aunt Faith. Learn to ski."

She might.

If Hudson asked her to, she would try it.

"So." He cleared his throat. "Moving to Nashville?"

"What?" She jumped to straighten in her chair and almost reached to close her laptop. The heat in her face now wasn't from embarrassment but guilt. "No."

"Mm-hmm." He nodded. "Which is why you were looking at teaching positions in the Nashville area."

Tori flinched and rubbed the bridge of her nose. The stress was beginning to give her a headache. Her parents would never let her starve if it ever came to that. But she wanted a job. She liked her independence.

That thought brought her back to Hudson again. Maybe she was rushing into this. Even just looking at job opportunities and housing in the Nashville area. What if he had no gumption to get out from under his parents' thumbs? What if he was comfortable in his misery? After all, he'd been in Montreal for a year and a half. Maybe living without control, without responsibility, was good enough for him.

Her first impression hadn't been terribly great if she remembered correctly. She'd thought he was pushy, asking for her charger, asking a second time when she didn't answer him immediately. He'd been messy, hair and beard unruly, like he'd rolled out of bed and pulled the joggers on and split. To hang out at a coffee shop and play games on his phone.

She didn't know him that well. How could she consider putting herself on a path that could lead to destruction with him? What about his brother? Beating up his girlfriend?

"Tori."

She snapped out of her thoughts. Her dad was watching her with that fierce, protective look only a girl dad knew how to do.

"You okay?" he asked quietly.

With a rugged sigh, she nodded and flopped back in her chair again. "Yeah. I'm good."

He stared a moment longer, as if he didn't believe her. When he finally looked away, Tori glanced at her computer and then at her phone. Was she being dumb? She and Hudson had talked almost every day since she had left Montreal. By all accounts, he was going to work every day. He looked and sounded professional, not like a bum living on his parents' dime by choice.

The sunset at her back reflected back to her in her screen, making her wish again that Hudson was here with her.

"I met someone."

Shocked by what had come out of her mouth, because what she thought she was going to say was that she had to consider a change in careers or locations, Tori and her dad simply stared at each other silently for several long moments.

"Good." Her dad finally nodded.

"But."

"But what?"

"I don't know, Dad. We had one day...one night...together. And then I had to leave. I don't know what to think."

"Was he good to you?"

A smile tugged at her lips. "Yeah. He was."

"Isn't that the most important thing?"

Maybe. Maybe not. Maybe his depression was a big thing. Maybe his drinking could end up a big thing. Maybe the fact that he let his parents control him was important.

"You'd think so," she said quietly.

"If you met him in Canada, what's that got to do with Nashville?"

Tori closed her laptop, picked up her wine, and started talking. She told him everything, except for the steamy, private details of their night together. She even told him about Liam Jones the soccer star beating his girlfriend, that Hudson's parents had bought her silence rather than trying to help Liam.

For a long time, when she stopped talking, her dad sat quietly. Thankfully, he wasn't watching her while he processed everything she'd said. Tori wasn't sure she could handle that.

"Did you talk to your mom about this?"

Tori snorted. "Um. Have you met Mom? She'd tell me to walk away. Relationships are overrated. And I should invest in the stock market."

Her dad laughed and shook his head. "No, she wouldn't, Tori. She would tell you to follow your heart."

"What?"

"She did. When she was younger. I did."

"And look at how that turned out." Tori took a drink.

"Look at how it turned out," he said with a deliberate nod in her direction. "Your mom and I loved each other so much. We had some great times, Tori. And we had you. Now we're the best of friends, we still talk, still laugh together. And we share a beautiful daughter."

Tori shifted her gaze, uncomfortable under his stare.

"Maybe by society's standards, we're in the failed marriage statistic. I don't care. Your mom doesn't care. She's a respectable businesswoman. I'm traveling and meeting people.

It may not be the life we thought we'd have when we got married, but neither of us has a single regret."

She huffed a sigh and dropped her head back to rest on her chair.

"But you'll never marry again."

"Nope. Don't need to. Your mother was the love of my life. It just didn't work out the way that it usually does. The women I see now? All wonderful, caring women. I know you think I'm a—"

She shook her head and squeezed her eyes closed.

"My point, Tori, is not everyone's happiness is the same. Unless you think this guy would physically hurt you—"

"No." She opened her eyes and stared at her dad boldly. "He wouldn't."

"Then follow your heart. You need to move to Nashville to give it a shot? Do it. You wanna move to Montreal so you two can give it a go there? Do it."

"It's a little soon for that."

He nodded. "Little soon to do it. Not too soon to consider what you want."

"Thanks, Dad," she said with a smile.

"Loni's making dinner. You gonna join us?"

She had been pleasantly surprised when she met Loni. The woman was closer to her dad's age than most of the women he had dated. And she was friendly and gabby without being too much.

"Yeah. I think I will. Thanks."

CHAPTER 23

HUDSON

His cell phone rang as the workday neared its end. Expecting it to be Tori, Hudson grabbed it, tapped the answer button, and then realized it was his brother on the other end of the phone.

"Hud."

"What?"

Hudson hadn't been lying to Tori about his brother. They had been close when they were very young, but the older they got, the further they drifted apart. With their parents' help. Liam's exceptional athleticism, particularly his soccer agility and skills, had been more important to the three of them than nurturing the sibling relationship between Liam and Hudson.

Mostly, Hudson thought Liam was a prick. And he avoided seeing him, unless it was a situation he couldn't get out of. Christmas dinner last year was one such occasion. Thankfully, it hadn't been a disaster, but it had been more like work than a fun family get together.

However, Hudson knew Liam suffered from depression. The same way he did. And he knew that his parents pushed it under a rug, insisting that Liam was fine. That there was nothing wrong with him that exercise couldn't cure. While exercise did help, Hudson knew from experience it wasn't always enough.

Liam wasn't a violent person. Something had driven him to drink too much and go after his girlfriend. Not another man. Hudson suspected it was the demon inside his brother that had done it. Not that it was an excuse. But it was certainly a red flag in Hudson's opinion. Liam needed help more than he did, and their parents had done him a disservice buying his girlfriend's silence.

"I need you to get over here. Now."

"I'm at work, Liam," Hudson reminded him. "Some of us have jobs with time clocks and regular hours."

Liam huffed on the other end of the line.

"It's almost five."

"Yes. Almost being the key word." Hudson stuck the phone between his shoulder and ear and focused his attention on the computer in front of him.

"Fine." Liam muttered something unintelligible. "Can you get over here when you're done?"

Hudson took his turn with a long sigh that ended in a growl. He had no desire to go visit his brother. But he would.

"What's up?"

One last ditch effort to get out of having to make the two-mile trip to his brother's place.

"She's talking. Mom and Dad are pissed. Takin' it out on me."

"What?" Hudson sat back in his chair and closed his eyes. Why was this his problem? Did he call Liam when he totaled his damned car? No. He hadn't called the first time, seven years ago. He hadn't been arrested for drunk driving that time, but he knew in his heart he shouldn't have been driving. What he would have given to be able to call Liam and vent to his big brother. He didn't call the second time he wrecked, either. Not even when he was released from the ER and left the hospital with friends. When his dad called to check on him, though his first words were something about how stupid can you be—

"Kelly's talking. Her sister dropped a hint to reporters last week about what really happened, and now they're all over her, pushing her to talk."

"She took the money Dad offered her—"

"Yeah, she did. What're they gonna do? Hire someone to take her out? No. And she knows that."

Hudson sighed and squeezed his eyes closed again.

"Look. I'll be over as soon as I get out of here."

He finished the financial statements he'd been working on for a local restaurant and then closed down his computer. Though he would much rather go straight to his apartment and get Tori on speaker phone while he cooked, he left his work building and headed in the direction of his brother's place.

It had been a month now since he met Tori. Since they'd had that one fun day together, freezing their asses off in the snow. His worries that they would drift apart as happens often in long-distance situations had faded away. But he still missed her. They talked every day, sometimes twice a day. And they wanted to see each other again—as soon as possible. So far, that timing hadn't worked out.

Tori had spent a week with her dad. Again, Hudson was happy she got to the spend that time with him and loved that she got to soak up sunshine while he was still walking in snow and slush. But he wished she could have stayed with him for that week.

Crazy. He knew that. Made more sense to do things this way. If she had stayed, they would have probably burrowed into his bed for an entire week or longer. He would have either had to leave her to go work or play hooky. Missing work right now was not part of his plan to get back out on his own. Nope, even though it sucked to be away from her, it was better to do things slowly. Let her find her way to some sort of work, whether she find a teaching position or get a fast-food job flipping burgers. He doubted it would come to that for her, but he knew she would do that before she sat around doing nothing.

She told him she was sending out resumes, filling in applications. She didn't say if she was looking just in Illinois or across the country. Hudson didn't ask. Yet. When he was back in Nashville, he might push his luck.

He buzzed Liam's apartment and yanked the door open when the lock clicked. It was warmer than it had been when Tori had been here, but it was still cold walking weather. Hudson unzipped his coat when the heavy door closed behind him. Still a little cold, he shivered as he crossed the lobby to the elevator. Liam lived on the fourth floor. Not a penthouse suite, but his apartment was twice as big as Hudson's. Made sense; Liam made bank on the soccer field. Nothing like he'd make in Europe, but more than Hudson was ever going to see in a year's time.

Liam's door was open when Hudson got off the elevator and headed down the hall. Hudson steeled himself when he heard his mother's voice. He should have known. The ice in her voice made him hesitate in the hall. Didn't make a difference that his parents were here to lecture Liam; Hudson didn't want to hear it. At the door, he grasped the trim with a white-knuckle grip and swallowed back the memories and the anxiety that always seemed to rear its head when he was around them.

"I can't believe she would do this," his father said. "After we gave her the money for the hospital bill. Even more than—"

Hudson clenched his teeth together and walked into the living room. Normally immaculate—Liam had a cleaning lady—the place looked like it had been ransacked. Dirty clothes, clean clothes, clothes Hudson was sure he'd never seen his brother wear, were tossed all over the floor and furniture. The coffee table was littered with take-out wrappers and empty beer and soda cans. A dirty plate with the remains of what appeared to be spaghetti crusted on it sat within a centimeter of falling off the table to the hardwood floor.

His parents, Hudson noticed, hadn't even sat down. Probably equal amounts rage and disdain over the state of the apartment. His dad stood at the far side of the apartment, arms folded over his chest, looking out the window. His mother stood near the sofa, hands on her hips, murder in her eyes.

Liam looked like hell. Curled up on the sofa in the fetal position. His hair stuck out at all angles, several days' worth of beard overtaking his usual clean-cut face. He wore sweats with a holey t-shirt. One dirty sock, the other foot was bare. Hudson recognized the look. He had been nearly identical just before he wrapped his car around the tree. His parents had no patience for mental illness. For anxiety or depression. They didn't get it; they didn't grasp the hell Liam was obviously in now any more than they understood what Hudson had gone through.

"This place is disgusting." His mom shot Hudson a look of reproach when she realized he was standing in the doorway. "What're you doing here?"

Hudson hesitated. He wasn't sure if he should tell them Liam had called or not.

"I asked him to come," Liam answered in a monotone.

"Well, you don't need to be here." She flashed another look at Hudson and waved a hand at him. "We're dealing with your brother's problem right now, so—"

"Are you, though?" he asked quietly. He took another few steps into the room, eyes moving from his mother to Liam.

"Excuse me?" She turned to him and tipped her head, clearly ready to read him the riot act for not just showing up, but also for having the gall to open his mouth and talk back to her.

"You're here to handle the Liam Jones and Kelly Kava scandal." Hudson shrugged.

"That's what I said."

"I'm here for Liam."

His dad decided now was the time to interject, so he turned from the window and sauntered across the room. "You think you know how to handle this, son? Should we put you in charge of the press?"

"I don't give a damn about the press, Dad," Hudson said simply. "I'm here for Liam."

Hudson felt Liam's eyes on him. Yep, his brother had turned into an arrogant prick through the years, but they had all let it happen. His parents because they were pushing him to be a superstar. And Hudson because he was bitter about being left behind. All of them had been selfish, but maybe Hudson most of all, since he understood the darkness that swallowed his brother up from time to time.

"Can you just go?" Liam croaked as he swung his legs over the edge of the sofa and sat up.

"See? Liam would like you to go."

Hudson arched his brows at his mom.

"I meant you and Dad," Liam corrected her. He stood; Hudson worried the pants he wore would slide to his ankles.

"I'm sorry. What?"

"Mom." Liam threw up his hands in desperation. "I hurt her. I broke her arm. I gave her a black eye. You don't fix that with money."

"We paid her hospital bill, Liam," his dad corrected him.

"Yeah, and then some. The then some is hush money. Because if my fans found out I did it, my career would hit the toilet. Well, guess what? My fans know. My career is in the toilet, and that's not even the worst of it."

Hudson flinched when Liam's voice broke.

"What's the worst of it?" Hudson asked his brother.

"I don't fucking care." Liam shrugged. "About any of it. About anything. I don't care."

"This again?" His mom rolled her eyes.

"Again?" Hudson barged further into the room, not sure if he was charging at his mother or stepping between them to defend his brother. "Again? You felt this way before?" He spun around to direct that question at Liam.

"All the fucking time." Liam ducked his head and rubbed his eyes with his fists.

"Liam, just take a shower. We'll get you some dinner, and we'll talk this over. We'll figure it out together."

Hudson glanced at his dad and then looked at Liam again.

"You're not gonna just figure this out—"

"Hudson, you have nothing to contribute here—"

"He is my brother!" Hudson snapped with a yell of rage. "He is my brother, and I know what he feels! I know what's going on in his brain—"

"I hardly think your life's regrets equate to what he's going through right now."

Hudson sucked in a deep breath. "Mom." He propped his hands on his hips to mirror her, still standing between her and Liam. "I say this with the utmost respect, but you don't have a fucking clue what I went through. What I still fight now and then. And you have no idea what Liam is feeling right now, either."

She shocked him with her silence.

"Look." Hudson breathed so deeply his nostrils flared. "Two days before I wrapped my car around that tree?" He turned a bit, eyes sweeping from his mom, over his dad, and finally to Liam. "I looked like that."

"You were drunk," his dad reminded him.

"I was." Hudson nodded. "Ever wonder why I was drunk? Why I chose to get in the car when I knew damned well I shouldn't be driving?"

Liam groaned softly and dropped to perch on the edge of the couch cushion. His father turned away from him, even though the depression, the mental illness he and Liam both dealt with, had come from his side of the family, from his own father.

When he swung his gaze back to his mother, she stared at him with bright eyes. Glassy eyes. For a moment, he was stunned to see tears in her eyes.

"Liam needs help." His voice was gruff now with emotion. "And by help, I'm not suggesting you throw more money at Kelly. I'm not suggesting you slap her with a lawsuit."

"I'm sorry."

Hudson turned to his brother when he spoke. Liam, still perched on the couch, looked up at him with bloodshot eyes.

"I didn't know, man."

Hudson shrugged and nodded. "I know. Because it's something we don't talk about enough in this family. In fact, the only time it's been talked about is when Mom wants to tell me I'm just lazy. That I'm too soft."

Liam scrubbed his hands over his face.

"Some people can't just pull themselves up by the bootstraps and snap out of it," Hudson looked at his mom again. "And there's nothing wrong with getting help for depression."

His dad moseyed back over to the window, but his mom took a few steps closer to Hudson. She touched his arm, squeezed gently, and then sat by Liam on the sofa.

"Is that true, Liam?"

"Yes, ma'am."

Hudson waited for her to say something dumb, like asking him why he'd never said anything. Why would Liam tell their parents how bad, how empty, he felt sometimes, when Hudson had been doing so for years and had been either ignored or chastised for it for years?

His mom rested her hand on Liam's shoulder and looked back at Hudson. It wasn't a hug, but then his parents didn't do a lot of that. Not with their sons. Not with each other. Still, it was something. Maybe the first step in a long journey.

She nodded. "I'm sorry."

Hudson took another deep breath and tucked his hands in his pockets. Still with his winter coat on, he was sweating by now. But he didn't want to stay. He would hang out here with Liam, if he needed him. But Hudson had no desire to stick around if his parents were going to stay.

"In my family," his dad frowned out the window as Hudson approached him, "you didn't talk about it."

"Well, we do now. And he needs help."

"And you?" His father turned toward him.

"I'm on medication," he answered simply. "Still have bad days, but the good days far outnumber them now."

Too refined, too strong and manly to speak, his father only nodded and looked away.

"Look." Hudson glanced over his shoulder at his brother and his mom. She had an arm resting on his back now. Hudson ignored the pang that sent through him. "I was planning to talk to you about moving back to Nashville."

"You sure you're ready for that?"

Hudson thought of Tori. Of the possibility of seeing her more often. Dating. Falling in love with her. Felt like he was halfway there already.

"I am," he said with a nod, "but he's not. I'm not gonna leave Liam until I know he's okay."

"And then?"

"And then I'm going home." Hudson shrugged. "I just want you to know that. I'm ready to take my life back."

Ready for whatever the future held for him and Tori. Now he just had to tell her that. He couldn't leave Montreal until he knew Liam, too, was back on his feet.

CHAPTER 24

TORI

Strange to accept a job offer and feel deflated and disappointed instead of excited. But that's how she felt. The job was even something she wanted; it wasn't in her exact field, but she would be teaching literature to junior high kids. She would still be working with kids, and that age group had its own set of issues and sharp corners she would have to navigate. She loved it for the challenge it presented to her, yes, but also because maybe she could make a difference for at least one child. Hopefully a classroom full of kids.

The trouble with the job was that it was in Illinois. Far enough away from her current town that she would have to move. But she would be no closer to Tennessee or Hudson if he ever got back to Nashville.

If it was possible to fall in love with someone over weeks and months of phone calls, after a one-day date that lasted over twelve hours, Tori was doing it. She lived for the cute text messages he sent her, the way he laughed at the silly jokes she sent him. She longed for evening to come, because they talked on the phone after dark. Sometimes, they got a little carried away with phone sex. But mostly, they talked. Shared their days. Their thoughts. The ups and downs. Their hopes to get together soon.

And now this. She had told Hudson she was looking for a job anywhere across the country. She hadn't come out and said she was definitely looking in the Nashville area, but he'd understood what she hadn't said.

Ready for a break after packing all day—she'd finally made a dent in her storage closet—she went to the kitchen to grab a cold drink. Pouring herself a glass of lemonade, she peeked out the kitchen window and noticed night creeping in. Wasn't full dark yet, but it would be within the hour. Might as well get this over with now. If Hudson had any plans to get back to Nashville soon, she wondered how long he would wait for her before he started seeing someone else. The guy was easy on the eyes, and the more she got to know him, the more she knew her first instincts about him were right. He'd made mistakes, bad decisions, either selfishly or out of self-preservation, but he was a good man at heart.

She took a drink of her lemonade and reached for her phone just as it rang. Flipping it over, she saw Hudson's face, that boyish grin that made her heart melt. This happened a lot— she called him just when he was about to text or call her. He called her just as she was thinking about getting comfortable to call him.

"Hey."

"Hi." His voice was warm and solid, like his hugs. She remembered the feel of his arms around her well, but she missed it. She wanted more of him. Funny thing was she had finally talked to her mom about Hudson, fully expecting her to roll her eyes and tell her to forget him. Expecting her dad to be wrong. But Tori was the one who had been wrong. Her mom had told her to follow her heart. And when Tori reported back to her dad about it, his words were *I told you so.*

She hadn't shown her dad a picture, but by the time she talked to her about Hudson, they'd been talking for six or seven weeks, and it felt a little different and sort of real. So she'd shown her mom a few pictures of Hudson.

Her mom had nodded her approval. God only knew what her dad might have done, since he did tend to relate to Tori on a whole different level than her mom did.

"I was just about to call you." She carried her glass and her phone to her living room and curled up in the corner of the couch. "I have news."

"I do, too."

"Oh! Good." Her stomach knotted. What if this was it? What if he told her he was moving back to Nashville and wanted her to consider moving there, too? Not moving in with him, not yet. Both knew that was rushing things. "You first."

"You sure?" he asked quietly. "Is your news good or bad?"

Worry ballooned in her belly now, so big and powerful it pushed her lungs, her heart, up into her throat. So far up she couldn't breathe.

"You go first," she insisted. Overall, her news was good, even if it meant they wouldn't live near each other yet. Something told her maybe Hudson's news wasn't good. What if he'd had an episode?

"Okay." He huffed out a quick breath and took a drink of something. On other nights, she would ask him what he was drinking. They would sit and talk as if they were in the same room together. Tonight, Tori sensed it wasn't a good time to play that game. "I'm gonna stay in Montreal for a while."

Tori swallowed hard and nodded, waiting for him to say more. When he didn't, her heart ticked up her throat in panic again. What did it mean that he wanted to stay in Montreal longer? That he didn't feel steady enough to be on his own yet? That he had been playing her all along, and that he was done with the game? With the phone calls? Ready to drop her and move on?

"Okay," she finally breathed the word, hoping he didn't hear the tremor in her voice.

"It's Liam," he told her.

A different sort of panic flooded her now, and she jumped off the couch to pace the living room.

"What happened? What's going on?"

"Um. Well, his ex—she broke up with him when all of that happened."

Even though he couldn't see her, Tori nodded, both for him to continue and in approval of Liam's ex walking away.

"I told you my parents paid her off."

"Yeah?"

"Her sister started dropping hints to the press. And they started hounding her. She eventually gave in and started talking."

"Even after accepting the bribe to stay quiet?"

"No honor among disingenuous people, I guess."

"Wow. How's Liam holding up?"

"He's not. And that's the problem."

"Hudson?" Her voice faltered. "What does that mean? Is he okay? Is he safe?"

"He's okay, but no, he's not okay. Wed had a blow up at his apartment yesterday."

"Yesterday?" she repeated. "Why didn't you tell me?"

"I had to process it," he mumbled. "And I was worried about how to tell you I was staying here."

"Okay." She nodded. She understood the need to process something like that; if anything happened to her parents or her aunt, she would be devastated and would need to get her head together before talking to Hudson.

"I...um." His hesitation made her flinch.

"What?"

"I think maybe you were right. When you asked me about the car and the tree."

Tori sniffled, her eyes burning now.

"And even though I was doing better, I think it took meeting you to see that. To face it. And to know I'm in a different, better, place now."

"Okay." Her heart raced, still in her throat. Her throat ached with the huge emotion she couldn't spit out and couldn't swallow.

"I talked to my parents."

"Good."

"I hope so. I hope they got it through their thick heads that Liam needs help. That ignoring the problem and throwing money at the results of the problem aren't the answer."

Throat still tight with tears she wanted to hide, Tori nodded. Her heart swelled bigger, proud of Hudson for standing up for himself and his brother.

"My dad's dad had depression. But they didn't talk about it then."

"I know."

"I just need them to understand that it's no different than treating diabetes or asthma. There's no stigma."

"I'm so proud of you." Her whisper was thick with pride. Joy, for him. Sadness that they would still be apart, even though she still had to tell him she wasn't leaving Illinois.

"I just want to stick around here for a while," he told her. "Make sure Liam gets treatment."

"I get it."

"I hate this, Tori. I'm ready to come back to the states. I'm ready to be happy. And I want you to be a part of my happiness."

The tears spilled, but she swiped at them and laughed. "Me, too, Hudson."

"Are you angry? I know I can't ask you to wait forever. You—"

"I took a job today."

"Shit. In Nashville?"

"How do you even know I was looking there?"

"Are you kidding me?"

"The job's in Illinois. So yes, I'll be moving. But no closer to Tennessee."

"I have an idea."

"What?" She had paced a good twenty circles in the living room. Breathless more with anticipation of Hudson's idea than the physical movement, she dropped to sit on the couch again.

"Come back to Montreal for a visit."

"Yeah?"

"We could do all the things we didn't get to do the first time."

"I have the suspicion that we'd be doing the same thing we did last time."

"Oh, we will most definitely be doing that again. But not before a night on the town."

Tori smiled so big her face hurt. "Is there still snow?"

"You hate snow," he reminded her.

"My dad may have convinced me it's not so bad."

"Will you come?"

She took a deep breath and flopped backwards. Propping her feet on the coffee table, she nodded. "On one condition."

"Name it."

"You'll come here, too. When you can. I want to show you my life, too."

"I promise I'll visit. Tori, I'll move to Illinois when I leave Canada, if it means we can see each other more."

"You don't have to do that."

"You have the roots. I don't right now."

He was right. Maybe they could put Tennessee aside for now. They could start in Illinois.

"Okay. I gotta get off the phone. Gotta book a flight and then empty my piggy bank so I can go to Montreal."

EPILOGUE

Hudson

Liam wasn't going to just miraculously get better. Hudson knew that; he still had good days and bad days. But things were slowly leveling out for him, and he was relieved that the wheels had finally come off for his brother. Hudson was grateful Liam had reached out to him and relieved that he had finally spoken his mind to his parents. They would never be the kind of parents Hudson wished he had, like his grandpa had been before he passed away. But this was something, a step in the right direction.

They were desperate for Liam to recover to get back on the soccer field. Hudson hoped that Liam would eventually be back on the field, doing what he loved. But above all of that, Hudson knew Liam had to remember who he was and how to love himself, how to find a spark of joy in himself, before he was ready to dive back into the spotlight.

Tori was on her way. Her flight had touched down about twenty minutes ago. Hudson wanted to meet her there, but she insisted she was fine with getting an Uber and coming to his place. He couldn't wait to see her. Talking with her over the last two months, texting and laughing, and lingering on the phone until all hours of the night—he loved every minute of it. But he couldn't wait to see her blue eyes and run his fingers through her curls again.

He took a look around the apartment, trying to see it through Tori's eyes. It was the same place, yes. But he had done some decorating. After all, he had made the choice to stay longer, to be around for Liam. And he had realized that refusing to settle in and feel at home here out of spite was only inconveniencing himself. He had asked his friends in Nashville to get some things from his storage unit and ship them to him. Not too much, because it was an unnecessary expense. So, now his living room had two pieces of abstract art hanging on the wall opposite the window Tori had stood before the one time she was here. He had purchased a couple of throw pillows for the couch—he had gone with navy blue for an accent color. And his favorite thing—he had printed a couple of the photos Tori had sent him since she left. A goofy, glitzy, touristy Montreal magnet now held them to his fridge.

Hudson couldn't wait for her to see the changes. And he was all for making more. Maybe they would find something together to stick in the empty living room corner—a plant or some piece of art. The thought made him laugh. Discount store art, maybe, for now.

He hurried to the door when he heard her knock. Yanking it open, he found himself looking at the face he had been dreaming about since she'd gone home. Her blue eyes were even brighter than he remembered. The grin on her face dazzled him.

"Hey." She quirked an eyebrow at him.

"Hi." He took a step toward her and gathered her in his arms. She had her bags with her. This time, she would be staying with him. Two nights, three days, just the two of them, alone together.

"You smell good." She nipped at his earlobe as she tucked herself into his embrace. "Wait. You look good, too. You clean up nice, Mr. Jones."

He laughed as she stepped back.

"Told you we're going on a real date tonight." He moved aside and took her bags so she could come inside. Tori shrugged out of her coat, eyes roaming over him from head to toe. He was glad he'd taken the time to make a dinner reservation and get the tickets for the AURA experience at the Basilica. And equally glad he had trimmed his beard again and dressed for her.

"Wow." She wagged her eyebrows at him and reached for his waist. Today the flat front pants were gray. His button-down shirt a deep, forest green. He felt much more himself and much more worthy of her attention, but he reminded himself often that she had been attracted to him on one of his less than great days.

"C'min. Let's get you settled."

She nodded but turned to hang her coat on the rack by the door.

"Oh my gosh, Hudson!" She gasped in surprise as she followed him into the living area. "This is great."

He watched her cross the room to study the artwork.

"I like it," she said with a nod. "Just this much feels like you."

"Good." He slipped his hands in his pockets. "I realized that I was only adding to my own misery, refusing to settle in and be comfortable here."

"Hmm." She peeked at him with a smirk. "How wise of you."

"Might have had a little push in that direction by a wise friend."

"Friend." She turned to him.

"Friend," he agreed, "though I hope we have more."

She laughed softly. "Pretty sure there's more."

He let her wander into the kitchen. Something weird swelled in his chest, his gut, when she saw her pictures on the fridge and let out a squeal of excitement.

"Wow." She turned to him again. "Guess what?"

"What?" He shook his head and closed the distance between them. Tori rested her hands on his shoulders.

"I put a picture of you on my fridge, too," she said with a grin. "But my magnet is from the Mark Twain Cave in Hannibal."

"Let's put that on our bucket list." He slid his hands down her sides and gripped her hips.

"We can do that."

Those blue eyes swept over his face and lingered on his lips again.

"Nashville can wait, Tori." His voice was gruff. "Nothing else matters right now. I just need to know you'll wait, too. I know long-distance relationships suck—"

Tori shook her head and pressed her fingers to his lips. "I'm here, Hudson. We'll make it work."

He tipped his forehead against hers.

"I need to freshen up and change for dinner," she told him.

"Okay."

He carried her bag down the hall to his bedroom and left her to get ready, as tempted as he was to follow her into the bathroom and the shower. Most of the snow from her first trip had melted, save for a few mountainous piles here and there in parking lots. The night was clear. They would walk to dinner and to the Basilica. Hudson couldn't wait to show her a beautiful, moonlit night in Montreal. He had come to like it here.

Wandering out through the living room, he stood at the window and watched the night settle in. He might like it here now, but Tori's eyes and smile lit up the night brighter than the moon and stars.

THE VAGABOND SERIES

A collection of standalone travel romances written by various authors you love!

Cruisin' to Cozumel by Amy Stephens

Jamaican Me Crazy Mon by Ireland Lorelei

Beached in Bali by Erin Brockus

Belize Bliss by C.L. Collier

Innocent in Istanbul by Heather E Andrews

Adventures In Honeymooning by Barb Shuler & KA Graham

Delayed in Venice by Margot Swan

Loving London by Tina Gallagher

Lost in Liberia by Saharra K. Sandhu

Moonlight in Montreal by Tracy Broemmer

Almost in Amalfi by Leigh Adams

Flirting in Fiji by A.M. Roark

The Singapore Stunt by Mel Walker

Delayed in Zurich by Margot Swan

Under Construction in Bora Bora by Jacie Lennon

Mai Tais and Goodbyes by J.A. Wynters

Delayed in Cape Town by Margot Swan

Broken Down in Ballyclare by Tina Gallagher

Finding True North by E.A. Pierce

A Polar Pursuit by S.E. Rose

Passion in Paris by C.L. Collier

Nights in Nepal by Tarrah Anders

Join the series' Facebook readers' group

Follow the series' Facebook page

Visit The Vagabond Series web site

ABOUT THE AUTHOR

Tracy Broemmer is the author of several contemporary romance novels including The H Books, Wedding Day Shenanigans, and the Mississippi Queen Trilogy. Tracy also writes women's fiction and is the author of the Williams Legacy series as well as several stand-alone titles.

Tracy's books have been called gripping, emotional, and timely, and readers describe her characters as real and relatable.

Tracy lives in Midwestern Illinois with her husband of 30 years. Visit her on the web and sign up for her newsletter at www.broemmerbooks.com

ALSO BY TRACY BROEMMER

Women's Fiction Novels:

Luther's Cross 10th Anniversary Edition

Fairytale (Writing as Therese Kinkaide)

Just Like Them

Small Hours

Picket Fences

Two Story Home

Green-Eyed Girl

Say Everything

Come Home For Christmas

Sketching Litchfield Lake

Ever, Again

Safe as Houses

Damsel

The Valentine Suite

Every Little Thing, Lorelei Bluffs, Book 1

Two A.M., Lorelei Bluffs, Book 2

Blind, Lorelei Bluffs, Book 3

Leaving July, Lorelei Bluffs, Book 4

Hesitation Marks, Lorelei Bluffs, Book 5

Four Letter Words, Lorelei Bluffs, Book 6

See Kate, Lorelei Bluffs, Book 7

Loved You More, Lorelei Bluffs, Book 8

A Lorelei Ending, Lorelei Bluffs, Book 9

I Do, Lorelei Bluffs, Book 10

Truth Is, The Williams Legacy, Book 1

Other People's Ugly, The Williams Legacy, Book 2

Omissions, The Williams Legacy, Book 3

Contemporary Romance Novels:

Destiny's Calling: Your Future Is Waiting

Wedding Day Shenanigans

Holiday Fling

The Kiss Off

Something Like Love

Plus One

Hold Onto the Stars, Book #5 in Blue Collar Romance series

The Jane Thing, Book #2 in Meet Cute Book Club series

Shameless Santa, Book #7 in Welcome to Kissing Springs series

Love, Nashville, The Mississippi Queen Trilogy, Book 1

Forever, Duncan, The Mississippi Queen Trilogy, Book 2

Always, Jess, The Mississippi Queen Trilogy, Book 3

Gettin' Hitched, The H Books, Book 1

Hookin' Up, The H Books, Book 2

Holdin' On, The H Books, Book 2.5

Contemporary Romance Novellas:

Indian Summer, A Novella

Dear Jaclyn Perris, A Novella

French Stuff, A Novella, Originally included in newsletter builder anthology, Just Coffee

Holdin' On, A Novella, Originally published in the anthology, Snowed Inn

End in Flames, Rescue Me Serial Anthology

Mistletoe Mishaps

Toasted: A New Year's Eve Novella

Endless Summer, Originally published in the anthology, Cool Off (Timberton Hounds)

Homeless Holiday, Included in the anthology, Let's Get Naughty (Timberton Hounds)

Deadman's Hollow

Boone's Girl, Originally published in the anthology, Aced, Back to School

Feels on Wheels, Originally published in the anthology, Fall Into Love (Love in Motion Duet)

Rings on Wings, Originally published in the anthology, Fall Back Into Love (Love in Motion Duet)

Intoxicate Me, A Novella (515 Whiskey)

Other Novellas:

The Devy Man, A Horror Novella

Women's Fiction Short Stories:

India Falls

Luther's Cross: 87,600

The Candy Cane Tree of Willow Lane

Delays, Originally published in the anthology, Snowed Inn, Vol.2

Same Time Next Year, Included in the anthology, Sweet Sprinkles

Contemporary Romance Short Stories:

Perfect Pictures, The Wine Tasting Series, Traminette

Coming Home, The Wine Tasting Series, Edelweiss

Save Me Every Dance, The Wine Tasting Series, Rosé

Marry Me, The Wine Tasting Series, Shiraz

Birthday Wishes, The Wine Tasting Series, Muscat

Dad Jeans, The Wine Tasting Series, Vignoles

Peppermint Lane, Originally published in the anthology, Sweet Treats

Priceless Memory, Timberton Hounds Sports Romance

Truly Dante, A Mississippi Queen Trilogy short, Included in the anthology, Naught & Nice

Strawberry Wine, Originally published in the anthology, Stand For Ukraine

Love Letter, Originally published in the anthology, Hope For Ukraine

Leaving You, A Lockland Distilling Short, Originally published in the anthology, Backing the Bluegrass

Sambuca Santa, Included in the NL Builder anthology, Kissing Santa Claus

www.ingramcontent.com/pod-product-compliance
Lightning Source LLC
Chambersburg PA
CBHW021054130626
46552CB00005B/2097